SO-BYY-665

TAILSPIN

Annabel Davis-Goff

Coward, McCann & Geoghegan
New York

Copyright © by Annabel Davis-Goff
All rights reserved. This book, or parts thereof, may not be reproduced
in any form without permission in writing from the publisher. Published
on the same day in Canada by Academic Press Canada Limited, Toronto.

Library of Congress Cataloging in Publication Data

Davis-Goff, Annabel.
Tailspin.

   I. Title.
PZ4.D266Tai   1980   [PS3554.A9338]   813'.54   79-17966
ISBN 0-698-11023-4

Printed in the United States of America

TAILSPIN

ALSO BY ANNABEL DAVIS-GOFF
Night Tennis

for Anthea

Chapter One

Diane woke up with a feeling of doom. No, doom was too dignified a word for it. That suggested dramatic circumstances beyond her control, made her a heroine or some tragic victim. And this was a self-inflicted wound. A feeling of nausea, a headache. Her mouth was dry and tasted awful; the skin on her face felt stiff. If she got up, took a shower, cleaned her teeth, took a couple of aspirin and had some coffee she'd have to feel better. But if she moved she might throw up. Another hangover. A cliché, a joke. But one that was lost on Diane.

But there was something else. The doomed feeling was not only physical. Half of her mind searched for the forgotten thing, going after it like a dream that seems important to remember, but is fading fast. The other half told her to wait until she felt stronger, until it could be jazzed up to seem funny. With repetition and some polishing, the almost certainly humiliating episode would become an anecdote. "Diane, tell them about the time when you . . ." But first she'd have to remember what it was. Odd that she couldn't; usually the horrors of the previous night hit her before she was fully awake.

Outside a church bell started to ring. It made her feel she

should be somewhere. But where? Maybe that was part of last night, too. More likely to be a leftover reaction to an Irish childhood. Ten minutes to get to church. The family gathering in the hall, prayer books, hymn books, last minute panic about gloves.

The telephone rang. Probably safer not to answer it. The ringing continued for longer than she expected, ten or eleven rings. Whoever it was knew she was there. It was something important. She got out of bed, made her way toward the telephone and was overcome by dizziness. She put her hand on the table to steady herself, and at that moment the ringing stopped. The church bells continued. Why? It was a weekday, of that she had no doubt. Shouldn't she be at work? What time was it, anyway? Light streamed in through the windows. No wonder she had a headache; she always did if she didn't sleep in a blacked-out room. Maybe the phone call had been from her office. No, that wasn't right. She didn't have to go to work. Never again. At least, never at her old job, but very soon somewhere else. She had to get up and find a job as soon as possible. Fired. Fired and broke.

The dizziness passed, but getting upright had suddenly made her feel worse. She rushed to the bathroom, held onto the basin with both hands, leaned over it and retched. She brought up some saliva—thick, yellowish and disgusting. She spat it out and turned the taps on.

Then she saw why she hadn't thrown up. She had earlier. Last night probably. And had cleaned up, thank God. Not well, but nothing that would take more than a moment or two, when she felt better. What the hell had happened last night? Her reluctance to remember some embarrassing and probably degrading incident disappeared into fear she would forget an entire evening of her life. If you were quick and smart and laughed a lot, you

8

could look people in the eye and pretend last night's drunkenness had been funny. But no one laughed at blackouts, lost nights. Lost nights? Scott Fitzgerald? Yes, but this, God help her, was more John O'Hara. Gloria somebody. And a bit about a toothbrush and a mink coat that she stole from the guy's wife. Funny she could remember that, and not know how she'd spent the previous night. For that matter, how did she know it was just one? It had to be. Today should be Friday. Friday. Good Friday. That was why the bells were ringing. But Friday was the end of the week; she had to go out and find a job, otherwise there was nothing she could do about it until Monday. And an apartment. This one had to be left by the end of the week. And cleaned up. Christ, if Jan could see her bathroom now.

Teeth brushing. Excedrin. A long shower. Shampoo. She got out of the tub, wrapped her head in a towel. No question of drying it, let alone setting it. She'd have to wear a scarf. Pity she'd fused Jan's hot curlers.

Coffee? No. Bloody Mary? Too dangerous. Better get back into bed, maybe sleep a little, give the Excedrin a chance. When she woke up she would remember everything, she'd feel better, she'd take decisive action, get an apartment. An apartment? A room would be more realistic, and a paycheck to rent it with. Otherwise she'd end in the gutter. The gutter. *Nostalgie de la boue* she'd said last night, and someone had laughed. Not kindly. A man, she thought. Why had she brought that phrase up? George had once said she was an example of it. Hardly flattering, but she'd been pleased, it had shown he'd been thinking of her, had some perception of her. Christ, she hadn't been talking about George last night, had she? That would be unbearable. But where had she been? A party, that bit she could remember fairly clearly. And then they'd gone out to dinner, or had been planning to go out to dinner. Seven or eight of them, something like that.

But that was as far as it went. She wasn't going to remember. She looked for her watch on the night table, but couldn't see it immediately. It seemed to be under the ashtray, stopped.

And in the ashtray was a cigar butt.

Well, now she knew. That certainly put a new perspective on it. No way of passing this off as part of the tragic heroine act. Plain unpleasant squalor. And if not remembering the night before was another first, a very scary step down, this was taking her a long way further. *Nostalgie de la boue* indeed, she'd sunk from the gutter to the sewer.

Her first instinct was, as usual, to run. To get out of here, not only out of the room, but the apartment, New York. In panic, she started to move fast. A robe, then something clean to wear. No sign of her purse. Where the hell was it? Could she have left it somewhere? Well, presumably whoever it was who'd brought her home and spent the night, part of it anyway, would have seen that she'd had her purse. Always assuming she'd come home with someone from the earlier part of the evening, the party, someone she knew socially. Someone she knew. But supposing it had been someone she met later?

The doorbell rang. It had to be him, coming back to murder her. Of course, if he'd stolen her keys, he wouldn't need to ring the bell, but she wasn't going to count on that. Not after whatever it was she'd done the night before. That was how you got murdered, or caught the clap. Or got robbed, as she evidently had.

Thank heaven for the intercom.

"Hello." She made her voice sound strong, discouraging.

"It's me. Sandy."

A girl's voice, pleasant, self-assured, not American. Not familiar. Sounded as though she were expected. Must be a friend of Jan's. Better let her come up, just keep her out of the bathroom, and the kitchen, and the bedroom for that matter. Diane pressed the buzzer to release the front door, turned to get her robe. Try to look as respectable as possible. Thank God she'd washed her hair; it made a good excuse for being in a robe at this hour of the day. And for getting rid of this Sandy person as soon as possible.

The intercom buzzed again.

"Yes?"

"I can't seem to get it open, I've got some stuff in my arms."

Diane pressed the buzzer for a good fifteen seconds, opened the door of the apartment, waited.

"Happy birthday," Sandy managed to lean over a large bunch of flowers, a bottle of champagne and a well-wrapped package to kiss Diane on both cheeks.

Happy birthday. Yes, well that was part of it. It filled in one clue, a piece of a jigsaw which didn't join any larger section. In the meantime there was this girl, this Sandy, to be dealt with. And all the things in her arms. Something had to be done. Too late. With a neat precise movement, a delicate well-shod foot pushed open the kitchen door. Diane closed her eyes, moaned almost silently.

"Oh, this is the kitchen. Good."

And she went in. Diane watched her helplessly, realizing nothing was to be gained by vague excuses like the maid hadn't shown up this morning. For some time she'd tried to persuade herself that fumigation and redecoration would do the trick, but she would now be ready to admit the only thing to do was to brick it up, carefully paper over the plaster and deny the apartment had ever contained a kitchen.

"Don't let me hold you up. Why don't you put your hair in rollers and I'll get some glasses and we can have a nice glass of champers."

Champers? Christ. And yet, this gave her an exit line.

"Lovely."

11

Putting her hair in rollers was perhaps a little ambitious for the moment. Her hands were too shaky, and raising her arms above her head seemed a minor acrobatic act. But she combed her hair and pulled it back in a rubber band. A big glob of cold cream was gratefully absorbed by her hungry skin. She was as ready as she was going to be.

There was a suspicious silence from the kitchen. What could be going on in there? If Sandy was, in fact, a friend of Jan's sent round to check the apartment perhaps she had fainted. On the other hand, maybe she was doing the dishes. Too quiet for that, though. Diane was more apprehensive than curious, and wavered outside the door for a moment. But the deciding factor was, though she was in possession of the vodka bottle, both the ice and the Bloody Mary mix were in the fridge.

Sandy was putting the final touches to the cake. She'd found a clean plate or, more likely, washed one. There was a doily under the cake, and some candles on it. When Diane opened the freezer for ice she found two glasses chilling there. And Sandy showed no signs of having noticed the squalor. She had just pushed it back a foot in either direction, like some explorer hacking a path through the Amazon jungle with a machete, well aware that given a day or two the vines and vegetation would grow over it, leaving no trace of his passage.

"Aren't you going to have champagne?" Sandy asked, watching Diane stir her Bloody Mary, adding an extra drop or two of Tabasco to get her circulation going. A slice of lemon would have been welcome, but that would have entailed a trip to a supermarket at some point within living memory.

"Absolutely. This is purely medicinal."

"It's a little early, isn't it?" Said with innocent curiosity, no hint of disapproval.

"I don't know," Diane said firmly, "my watch stopped."

Sandy seemed to accept this non sequitur as a satisfactory explanation, and nodded. There was a short pause, and Diane remembered that she still had no idea at all who this girl was. But since she knew herself to be suffering from at least partial amnesia, it was perhaps wiser not to come straight out and ask.

"Let's go and sit down." Get out of the kitchen. The not so faint, unmistakable smell of garbage was counteracting the healing effects of the Bloody Mary.

In the tiny hallway Sandy picked up the gift-wrapped package.

"This is from Sarah." And as Diane continued to look baffled: "Your sister. Oh, sorry, I should have explained. You must think I'm barmy. I'm a friend of Sarah's. When I said I was coming to New York she asked me to mail your birthday present. But I thought I'd bring it over in person. The cake and champagne are from me."

"Thank you. How sweet of you." And it was. This girl, this child, she couldn't be more than eighteen, was certainly kind, however poor her timing might be.

Diane smoked her first cigarette and finished her drink, and felt immediately and dramatically better, though still well below par. And par had been on a lower level in the last few weeks. She took quick stock of the situation. She still had to do something constructive about her immediate future, but first she had to get rid of Sandy, who seemed to be settling down. Well, some small social effort was required.

"So. How's Sarah?"

"She seemed terrific."

"And her new job?"

Sandy looked blank.

"She didn't say."

Odd that a friend of Sarah's shouldn't know about the new job. Even Diane had had pages on the subject, and she and Sarah weren't particularly close.

"Still living in St. John's Wood?" This was a sort of test question.

"I suppose so." Sandy answered, vaguely.

Diane opened the package. A Shetland sweater, a nice, useful, welcome present. Typical of Sarah, who always sent things she mistakenly thought unavailable in the United States. And a card, in Sarah's handwriting. So this girl did know Sarah a little, though obviously she was not actually a friend. Probably had met her at a party or something. In which case, why this vast production? A little more questioning seemed in order.

"And what're you doing in New York?"

"Oh, just passing through. I wanted to go to California, and I thought I might as well spend a couple of days in New York. I've been camping with a girl friend."

"What do you do? For a living, I mean."

"Oh, nothing for the moment. I was working in an art gallery in Bond Street, but it got frightfully boring."

Not employed, going to California, very expensively dressed. Lovely cashmere sweater, very expensive handbag with a Hermes scarf carelessly knotted through the handle. Yet apparently Sandy was camping with girl friends. But suddenly it all became clear.

"Is this flat all yours, or do you share?"

She was looking for somewhere to stay. Fairly urgently, too, if she was considering slumming it here.

"It belongs to a friend, I'm just moving out."

"Oh." No sign of disappointment from Sandy, almost an air of relief.

"Listen, the champagne and . . ."

"Oh, yes, of course." And Sandy leapt to her feet.

"No, I meant . . ." And Diane had to trot after Sandy who was returning to the kitchen. "I meant, it's sweet of you, but can you afford it?"

14

"Oh, that's all right. I charged it to Bob's account. I'll settle up with him later."

Diane tried to think of a single occasion in her life when she'd been in a position to charge anything to anyone's account, yet this self-possessed child seemed to regard it as a normal fact of life. You could see most things came easily to her.

And now she had to face cake and champagne and the squalor of the kitchen. If Sandy hadn't been there she'd have had another Bloody Mary, but she didn't want to be simultaneously judged both drunken and dirty. And there was something shiny clean about Sandy.

"Cleanliness is next to godliness," she found herself saying.

Sandy's head whipped around and she laughed.

"Did they say that to you at school, too?"

"Of course." And Diane started to remember. "And on speech day the School Matron used to get up rather pink and embarrassed by being a nonacademic which at my school was a laugh, and make her standard speech on the subject."

"Us too. Only ours was a nun, of course. And did you all cheer and clap too much?"

"Absolutely. It was eagerly awaited. The high point of the whole proceedings. You're a Catholic?"

"Yes."

"You're an English Catholic and I'm an Irish Protestant. We both seem to be the wrong way round."

Diane glanced at Sandy, realizing that her remark about cleanliness hadn't been prompted by the dirt around them but by an association to her boarding-school life. Suddenly she knew who Sandy was. She would have known sooner had her brain not been clouded by the excesses of last night and Sandy's presence being so out of context. Sandy was a "Northerner." Not literally, of course. Diane had attended a boarding school in the south of Ireland. It was run on English lines, and attended by southern

15

Irish-Protestant girls whose parents couldn't afford to send them to school in England, and by more affluent girls from the north whose parents sent them south hoping, usually in vain, that they might modify their accents. They were the girls who owned angora sweaters, Pringle twin sets, had fathers who added one cultured pearl to their necklaces each birthday and Christmas, lived in the certainty of a modest mink stole for their twenty-first birthday. Their suburban homes were far less beautiful than the crumbling Georgian house that Diane's family lived in, but easier to heat, cheaper to run and far more comfortable. These girls went on an annual holiday to a hotel, sometimes abroad. They were allowed to date mildly. Diane didn't think them sophisticated, nor did she envy them their clothes. But they made her aware that her own were usually hand-me-downs from Sarah, and that Sarah had not always been given them as new. Often they'd been expensive clothes passed on from a richer cousin. It was just that the lives of these girls seemed more up-to-date, more modern. Easier. In their backgrounds no one was being sacrificed in the struggle to maintain a family house with a leaky roof. They had no interest in, nor were they impressed by, old families, tradition. Nor higher education. These girls, or the English equivalent that Diane was soon to meet, had no aspirations or ambitions in that direction. During the three years Diane had spent at Oxford, struggling to survive on an inadequate allowance, she had met their kind again. They'd attended secretarial colleges, not from a burning desire to become proficient in the minor arts of shorthand and typing, but to have a good time, to go to dances and balls, possibly to marry some well-connected undergraduate. If not now, later, when they moved to London and shared flats in South Kensington. Taking jobs, not in publishing, but at Sotheby's or Christie's or working in an art gallery. They were all subsidized by allowances from home, and worked at places where they would meet husbands. They shopped together,

16

lunched together. Always had pretty clothes and married young. Try as she would, Diane could never feel superior to them. She had intelligence, birth and education. They had Vidal Sassoon haircuts, expensive shoes and boyfriends. She never lost the feeling that somehow they'd worked it all out properly and she was the one out of step. For a time she watched them and waited for disillusionment to set in, to see one or two of them fall on their faces, but instead she was the one who started to come apart.

And here was another of them. Ten years younger than herself. And in a strange country. If Sandy was really maintaining her edge here, where Diane was failing so miserably, it had to prove something.

Diane found herself, while in no way warming to the idea of the cake, really glad Sandy had turned up. She was someone familiar, and it was a comforting feeling. The aura of security and confidence that surrounded Sandy made Diane feel better. She realized just how starved she was for that particular kind of company, for someone who would even know what she was talking about if she remembered a boarding-school incident. To her surprise she found she liked this girl. Her ease and charm and English accent were a reminder that there was another life besides the dirt and misery and depression and endless dog shit on the streets of New York. And she thought she could learn something from her.

She started to smile again at the memory of the School Matron who, in day-to-day school life was referred to as "Nurse," a word which she herself pronounced "Narse."

She was just about to tell Sandy about it when she saw her purse. Among the dishes. God knows how it had gotten there. She picked it up, opened it to check if her keys were there, and found inside a great wad of money.

"I'd better put these flowers in water," she heard Sandy say, as though from a great distance.

Angling herself away, Diane took a closer look at the money. There seemed to be about five hundred dollars. A windfall, a godsend, but from where? Or whom? It was always possible that during the forgotten hours of last night she'd gotten into a poker game, or won a bet, or been on a television game show, or been adopted by a rich eccentric. Possible but not probable. What was probable though, was this . . . this roll was connected with the cigar butt. Which meant she'd been given money by a man. Or, if you were being picky about it, paid. But for what? What in the name of God could she have done to warrant five hundred dollars? A man who smoked cigars in bed and carried a lot of cash. Sounded as though she'd broken into the Mafia. Another great leap downward.

"Do you have a vase for these?"

"What?"

"Something tall and narrow?"

She closed her purse carefully and turned toward Sandy, who stood amidst, but apparently oblivious to, the squalor. Holding the flowers, their stems newly cut and crushed. White flowers. Appropriate for Sandy, certainly not for her as she felt at the moment. Making a giant effort, Diane reached up to a cupboard above the sink, in the back of which she thought she remembered seeing some flower vases.

As Sandy ran some water into the vase and rinsed out the dust, Diane poured them both another glass of champagne, aware that this third drink on top of the residue of last night's was making her slightly drunk again. It didn't matter. Obviously today was not one for job hunting. And she had to deal not only with the series of shocks she's received in the last hour, but with this girl, whose youth, beauty and look of innocence were underlining the squalor of Diane's surroundings and her life in general. Things were moving faster and more out of control than usual. But within part of the problem lay part of the solution. Five hundred dollars was five hundred dollars and now Diane had a plan. She'd run away. As she had many times before. Without actually dropping out of Oxford—in fact she'd got a fairly good degree— she'd run away from the life, from her friends, from the expected continuity of achievement. And from London, a year later, she'd continued her flight. To New York and the mess she now found herself in. And now . . . She glanced at the money again. It was hardly going to take her to California. But it should be enough to get her across the park.

Chapter Two

Most men lead lives of quiet desperation. So do many women, of course. But not Claire. The first time Diane saw her she was beating the shit out of a Tampax vending machine in the john of a First Avenue singles bar.

"Take that, you neo-fascist bastard," she screamed, battering it with a high-heeled shoe.

"Can I help?" Diane was curious; it was hard to ignore what was going on. Difficult to just pee, powder one's nose and leave as though it were an everyday sight.

"I don't know." Claire considered the question seriously, though not pausing in her onslaught. "Do you have a tool or weapon of any kind? An ice pick? Screwdriver?"

"No, but I could let you have a Tampax if that would help."

"Thanks, leave it on the counter. I just want to finish this thieving cocksucker off."

The door opened and for a moment Abba sang "anybody could be that guy" and then it closed behind a tidy blonde, just the kind to call the management and complain there were vandals in the ladies' room. Diane left quickly.

Twenty minutes later she glanced at her watch. Alone, and likely to remain so. The drinks here cost a fortune and she hadn't come here to get drunk. That would come later; she'd pick up a bottle on the way home. She'd come here to meet people. To meet a man, men. So had the other single girls. But they'd come in neatly matched pairs or, if alone, accompanied by a certain kind of confidence Diane had never seen in English girls, the confidence earned by exercise class, the women's movement, *Cosmopolitan* magazine, expensive clothes and haircuts, a career. They all had careers; Diane was the only secretary she knew. Nowadays the youngest, the least competent of these girls called herself somebody's assistant. Diane called herself a secretary, and she was twenty-six, somewhere between the pretty young girls and the heavily streaked, tennis-fit older women. But the tennis women had a different aura about them. Alimony confidence, probably willing to buy the next drink for a man who came on to them, guaranteed lays. They, like Diane, had a hungry look, but their hunger was identifiable, could be dealt with. Diane's was scary.

And yet Diane knew she had to make the effort. She was falling back on the superstition that if one went enthusiastically to ten hopeless parties, God would give one marks for it and at the eleventh one would meet Someone. But in her heart she knew that eleven more visits to this bar would not pay off. Another fifteen minutes, if she could nurse her drink that long, and she would go home. Someone sat down beside her. It was the crazy girl from the john.

"Okay if I sit down?" she asked, making herself comfortable, opening her purse and taking out cigarettes.

"Sure."

"I mean, if you're waiting for a late date I promise I'll split as soon as he arrives, and I won't even drop a scented lace Kleenex or my telephone number."

"No, really, I'm alone. I was just going."

"Stay a few minutes. I'll buy us a drink."

"Well . . ."

"Don't be scared. I'm not making a pass."

Diane was now totally confused.

"I didn't for a minute think . . ." she mumbled.

"Good. So . . . waiter . . ."

To Diane's amazement a waiter materialized immediately, took their order, left.

"That was impressive."

"Man over beast. What they're really trying to do is humor me, hoping I'll pass out quietly before I go berserk."

"But what about your date? Or are you here by yourself?" It didn't seem likely. This wasn't a girl who did anything on spec.

"He's with a bunch of the dullest people I ever met and that's saying something. Of course, he's no prize himself."

"But . . ."

"But if he's so awful, what's someone as wonderful as me doing with him? Well, he's a great lay," Claire replied, not lowering her voice by one decibel. "And as you can probably work out for yourself, I just got the curse. I mean, I don't have anything personal against vending machines. I was just taken short. And Hank doesn't like to do it in those circumstances. You know, I think I could forgive almost anything in a man who doesn't mind fucking when I've got the curse."

Diane looked around her nervously, aware they were attracting sidelong glances, not necessarily of admiration, from the group at the next table.

Fortunately the drinks arrived and Claire was, for a moment, diverted. Diane glanced at her watch again, decided to gulp down her drink, which had been very welcome, and go.

Within a week they were sharing an apartment.

22

A grim, rather dark apartment. Too far up and too far east for absolute safety and certainly not fashionable. But the kind something could be "done with." Neither Diane nor Claire "did" anything with it. They hit the bed linen department at Gimbels, opened an account at the local liquor store, and considered the place made over. And, as Claire said, if you didn't mind tearing open a cute little paper container every time you wanted salt, pepper, sugar or cream, and if you liked drinking miniatures, working in the airlines made a lot of sense. Diane did, however, draw the line somewhere.

"I'm grateful, really, for those First Class disposable prepowdered jobs, but I like the security, I suppose you might call it, of my own personal familiar toothbrush. I may be very old-fashioned, but I'd rather go to the drugstore and invest what remains of last week's pay in a real toothbrush and paste. You're not offended, are you?"

"*I* may be very old-fashioned, but surely a girl who nearly got a whatya call it, First in English, can do better than be a badly paid typist to a third-rate writer."

"He's not third-rate."

"How do you know? Have you read anything of his?"

"Sure I have."

"I mean before you worked for him."

"No."

"Well, then."

"There are lots of perfectly respectable American writers I haven't read. They weren't required reading at Oxford. He ain't Chaucer, you know."

"I'll say."

"Don't be catty. Have you ever read him?"

"Philip or Chaucer?"

"Either."

"Can't say I have. You know my speed. Doctor and nurse

23

romances. It's an airline rule. If they catch you reading without moving your lips it's a warning. If they catch you twice you're out."

"So what've you got against him?"

"He's taking advantage of you, that's what."

"No, he isn't. I'm an illegal immigrant. I'm lucky not to be washing dishes or picking grapes. And I can hardly ask my last employers for a reference. What could they say? 'A damned good editor, unfortunately we had to let her go for drunk and disorderly and weeping on the job.' I'd rather take my chances of working my way up."

"You see chances of promotion?"

"No, but . . ."

"Oh, I see . . ." And in Claire's expression there was both comprehension and disapproval. "You're sleeping with him. I might have guessed."

"I am not."

"Why not? At least that'd be something."

"Well, for one thing, he hasn't asked me, and for another . . ."

Diane tailed off. Conversations with Claire often confused her. Claire was uneducated, terrifyingly literal, relentlessly anti anything that smacked of the intellectual. And yet . . .

Diane felt she knew more about the whole Philip thing than she had any right to. Philip. She was wrong about his writing, there was no question of that. Philip Hope was a good writer. The critics liked him, his fellow writers respected him, the man in the street knew him from his first, brilliant, commercially successful war novel. They thought of him as a man's writer, but women were drawn by his photograph on the back of the book. Diane, who had spent enough time in publishing and who had a healthy streak of cynicism, knew just how carefully that photograph had been chosen. Taken in Vermont on the farm where

24

he'd lived before he'd made it big and moved to New York. His smile, his intelligent, slightly lined face, the streaks of gray in his thick dark hair. The sheep dog at his side. The photograph still adorned the jacket of the six or seven books he'd written since he'd moved to a brownstone in the East Seventies. Even so, Diane reacted to it just as strongly as his most devoted fan. And Claire was right about that. That was why Diane stuck around in an unrewarding job. She was a little in love. And anyway, apart from that, it was better to earn less and be on the distant fringes of a literary job than typing invoices.

Which left Claire's question unanswered. She wasn't sleeping with him. Why not? He slept with everyone else. What was wrong with her? There was a seemingly endless stream of girls coming to the house. Most of them younger and prettier than Diane, but not all. Most of them terminally silly, but even there an exception or two could be found. Probably just as well her fantasies stayed fantasies. She couldn't afford to sleep her way out of this job.

"And for another. . . . ?" Claire wasn't one to allow an argument to go unfinished.

"And for another I'm not really sure that being a parlor maid in the sky is necessarily a better job."

Claire raised her eyebrows and assumed a smug expression. "Oh, yes it is. Fly me, I'm Claire. And think of the perks. So, are you coming to the airport with me or not?"

"I don't think so, but thanks."

"Snob."

"No, I'm not."

But she was, a little. Claire's stories of life behind the scenes in an airline made Diane laugh, but even so she didn't want a blind date with a steward.

"So, come. I'll get you a ride back afterward. You don't have to screw the guy, for Christ's sake. You couldn't even if you wanted to unless he stowed you away on the flight to Singapore. It's just a drink."

"I'm going to a movie."

"Black and white and subtitles, right?"

"Yes."

"You just don't want to have fun. All right, keep the home fires burning until Tuesday. And *write down* all my phone calls."

The telephone started to ring thirty seconds after Claire left the apartment. Diane obediently picked up a pencil and pad as she went to answer it, following the four-mile extension cord into the bathroom, where Claire had left it. The pencil and paper came in handy, but the call wasn't for Claire; it was Philip, with an urgent letter on his mind.

Diane was glad Claire wasn't home. Then she'd have had the additional pressure of Claire making faces and wind-it-up gestures while she took dictation. No easy task since she was in mid-manicure.

This semivoluntary unpaid overtime was typical of Diane's job. She tried to conceal it from Claire, along with the fact that almost half her secretarial job was dishwashing and light housework, that her lunch hours usually included collecting his dry cleaning or some similar errand.

"Got it? Thanks, you're an angel. Just wanted to get it in the mail tonight and I'm on my way out to a movie."

Diane was no longer on her way out to a movie. She was scribbling desperately, trying to remember the closing sentence and to protect the wet nails on her left hand; she's already given up on the right. The phone rang again.

"Hold on a moment, please."

She wrote down what she thought Philip had said. More or less. Shorthand wasn't her strongest point. Being a secretary had never really been in her plans. Unfortunately, as it now turned out.

26

"Sorry . . . hello . . . who?"

Sandy. Who the hell was Sandy?

"Hi, Sandy. How are you?"

"Fine. The thing is, I just got in from L. A., and I'm at the airport."

"Yes," Diane said, cautiously.

"Well, I haven't anywhere to stay yet, and I was wondering if you could put me up?"

Oh, that Sandy. That was the trouble with putting your name in the telephone book. But interesting men you met at parties couldn't be trusted not to lose the envelope which had your number on the back.

"Well, we just have this tiny apartment, but Claire's away so if it would help you for tonight . . ."

One hour and fifteen dollars later (Sandy didn't have any change) Diane was helping Sandy carry an improbably large amount of luggage upstairs.

"What're you doing in New York?"

"Well, I was on my way back to London, and then I thought, the weather being so foul there at this time of year and no one really being about, I thought I'd stop in New York on my way back, see some friends, maybe get a job and spend the winter."

See some friends. Odd she hadn't made arrangements to stay with them, or at least called them before calling Diane. But there seemed no gracious way to ask about that.

"What kind of job? Do you have a green card?"

"Green card?"

"You need a work permit to get a job. What does your visa say?"

"I don't know. I mean, I got a six-month visa at the American Embassy. I have an old friend who works there . . ."

"But Immigration. What did they say at the airport when you first arrived in the States? You know, in spring."

"They asked me what I was doing and I said I was on holiday. They stamped my passport for one month. Jolly unfair. But I can always apply for an extension."

Of course she could always apply, but it wasn't likely her request would be granted. Diane started to feel worried about Sandy. She hoped there was a return ticket to London in all that luggage.

"But you can't get a real job without a green card. What were you thinking of doing?"

"Oh, I don't know. I thought I'd take a look around and see what there was. How do you manage, about a work permit, I mean?"

"Well, I work for a writer, he pays me cash, declares me as casual labor."

"You see. It's not impossible."

No, of course not. It wasn't impossible, but Diane couldn't imagine Sandy as a secretary. Well, Sandy would have to work that one out for herself.

"Now, if we stack the ones you won't need for the night over here . . ."

Now was the time to make it very clear this was just an overnight stop. Already she was beginning to feel responsible and guilty, a monster about to turn a kitten out into the rain. But she wasn't qualified to deal with Sandy's life as well as her own. Surely Sandy must have had some kind of fall-back plan when she arrived. She thought of Claire and made herself sound firm.

"I'm afraid you'll have to sleep in Claire's bed—she's away for the moment. But she'll be back tomorrow. Or the day after," she added weakly.

"Oh, that's fine. What a nice apartment, can I see the rest?"

"There isn't much rest. There's barely enough room for the two of us. The bathroom's through here."

"Lovely. I'll just put this bag in the bedroom and then we'll have a lovely chat. I'm dying to tell you all the latest gossip."

As far as Diane knew, Sandy and she had no acquaintances in common. Sandy was treating her like her oldest friend and it wasn't a reassuring feeling.

No doubt about it, Sandy made the apartment into a home. A rather small home, but pretty. Not everyone would appreciate the living room becoming Sandy's boudoir, but she'd made it look nice. All closet space had long since been exhausted, but Sandy had a way of hanging articles of clothing around the room that made a pleasant effect, especially the hats and the boa and strings of beads. Diane had gotten used to it, and she rather liked it. Claire didn't.

The kitchen was changed too. Before Sandy's arrival the fridge was a brief resting place for wine and beer, and occasionally food designed to be eaten directly from the container while standing up. Now there were regular meals, a proper breakfast. Diane enjoyed them too, but Claire was furious.

"Toast or muffin?" Sandy called through the bathroom door to Diane, who was putting her hair in hot rollers. She tended to spend more time and care on her appearance to go to work for Philip than she did when she occasionally went out in the evening.

The muffin was golden crispy and running with melted butter, and Diane was about to sink her teeth into it when Claire put her head around the door.

"Diane, could you give me a hand with something?"

Diane got up reluctantly.

"Time for another cup of coffee, Claire?" Sandy asked sweetly.

"No, thanks. I'm late already."

Diane followed Claire into the bedroom, closed the door behind them. Claire looked furious, her rage lent authority by her airline uniform.

"Okay, I'm going now. And by the time I get back I want her out or paying rent *and* her share of the groceries. There's only room for two in this apartment. And if we have another body here it's going to be a tenant, not a fucking *wife*."

"All right, I'll talk to her," Diane said weakly.

"And next time a stray dog or lame duck phones you from the airport, refer it to the zoo."

"Come on, she's only a kid."

"So were Leopold and Loeb." Claire seemed to be warming to her subject, but the telephone rang. All three girls reacted like Pavlov's dogs. Diane and Claire sprinted for it, but Sandy beat them to it by a nose.

"Oh, hello. No, this is Sandy. I'm just staying here . . ." Her voice was decidedly seductive. Both Claire and Diane glared at her. "Oh, here she is. Claire, it's for you."

She handed over the telephone to Claire and sat down again at the breakfast table. Diane looked her over with less than her usual generosity. Sandy looked the picture of youth and innocence. Her very slightly made up face and shiny hair could have been on the cover of any semi-sophisticated adolescent magazine. She made Diane think of a nursery expression: butter wouldn't melt in her mouth. And yet she tended to bend, without actually breaking, the rules where the other girls' male visitors were concerned. Bright and friendly, never anything you could put a finger on or tackle her about. But she got more than her fair share of attention from the other girls' dates. Not that it had mattered so far, but the day might come . . .

". . . no one . . . just a friend of Diane's who's staying here for a few days." Claire laid heavy emphasis on the last four words, and after an affectionate good-bye, put the receiver down and turned to Diane.

"That was Ted, he's coming Saturday." She glanced at Sandy. "Well, I'm off. Diane, remember what I told you. Good-bye, Sandy. If I don't see you again, have a good time in New York."

Sandy would have to go, that much was clear. Fond of her though Diane had become, there could be no question of her being there when Ted arrived. She had two days to get her out. If Philip was busy, she would call some friends who might be conned into putting Sandy up for a while. It was either that or taking her out onto the Cross Bronx Expressway and dumping her. If only she wasn't so trusting and helpless and so goddamn young.

But Philip wasn't busy. When she arrived at his house in the East Seventies, he was waiting in the hall looking aggrieved.

"Thank God you're here." The inference being she was late, though she wasn't. "Heidi's quit."

"When? Why?"

"God knows. Last night."

No real surprise there. Diane had never figured Heidi as a stayer, but had hoped the arrangement would last more than a week this time.

"I'll call the agency, but I'd better tidy up a bit first. Have you had breakfast?"

"Phoebe fixed it."

Phoebe was this week's girlfriend. Diane started off toward the kitchen. This was part of the usual morning routine. She made coffee for Philip. (He fancied himself rather a connoisseur.) After that they opened the mail, Philip dictated any letters he might have, then retired to his study to work. If he were between housekeepers, which was the usual state of play, Diane straightened up, went to the market and served his lunch on a tray promptly at one-thirty.

The kitchen looked as though a partially trained ape had been

31

allowed to try to prepare a meal. Diane said nothing, and pulled on some rubber gloves. Philip, standing in the doorway, looked at the scene with mild distaste and turned to go.

"Oh, yes, and send her some flowers."

"All right."

"And use another florist. The last place you used sent her a cactus."

Only because Diane had been unable to lay her hands on a Venus's flytrap.

"What do you think Phoebe would like?" he asked.

"Birds of paradise." They were the ugliest flower Diane could think of offhand.

"Fine. Do that and call the agency, then let's get on with the mail."

Diane loaded the dishwasher, set it in motion and took out the garbage. The rest could wait till later. She called her friend Lloyd who ran a flower shop, feeling mildly guilty because her malice toward Philip's girls would soon lose him a customer. And also because she had a favor to ask.

"What'll it be this time? Skunk cabbage or poison ivy?"

"No, we'll have to cool it for a while. The little pet complained about the cactus. But I got him to say yes to some birds of paradise."

"She'll probably love them. All right, I'll get them off this afternoon. Got to go now, this is a busy day."

"Wait a minute. I meant to talk to you about that. Your problem is you're understaffed and I've got a friend who . . ."

Suddenly it seemed as though the day might turn out all right after all.

When Diane arrived home Sandy was wearing a robe. Not the one she'd had on when Diane had left for work. It wasn't that she lounged about all day without getting dressed. As far as Diane could make out Sandy got up slowly, pottered about the apartment, went to the market or out to lunch, and did a little mild decorative food preparation. Often when Diane came home there was a little tray of hors d'oeuvres and a pitcher of martinis ready mixed. All quite pleasant activities, but Diane couldn't imagine them filling two hours of her day and, for Sandy, they seemed to be a full-time occupation. Now she was back in a robe, getting ready to go out. The bathroom door was open, filling the tiny apartment with steam and the sound of running water. Fortunately Claire wasn't there to complain about the tropical jungle atmosphere.

"I called the drug store, we were nearly out of Vitabath, I hope you don't mind . . ."

This was just the kind of thing that Diane did mind, and that drove Claire crazy. Diane did without Vitabath and Claire sometimes bought it duty-free. Sandy considered it a necessity of life, about on a par with toilet paper.

"No, that's all right," Diane said, not wanting to get diverted. This one last time wouldn't hurt. The thing was not to launch into a lecture on poverty and extravagance, but to have a serious talk with Sandy before she disappeared into the bathroom for an hour and a half.

"I ordered a few other things we needed at the same time."

Oh, well, maybe it was just toothpaste. If not, and they hadn't been unwrapped, perhaps they could be returned.

"Listen," Diane said, taking the chilled glass Sandy offered her, lighting a cigarette and positioning herself between Sandy and the bathroom door, all at the same time. "I have a friend who runs a little flower shop, he's looking for an assistant . . ." No, that was a bit strong. ". . . I suppose really more of an apprentice. I thought it might be just the thing for you. I mean, if you haven't come across anything better."

33

Come across was almost the word for it. Sandy had never actually, as far as Diane could make out, looked for a job. She had just been prepared to take one if it presented itself favorably to her. But she looked pleased.

"Oh, Diane, you angel. I'd love it. It's just the kind of thing I'm good at. Thank you, thank you."

"Well, it won't be very glamorous at first, you know, just a lot of running around and fetching and carrying. But if you stick to it, it could lead to something."

Without scaring Sandy off, Diane was trying to close the gap between Sandy's image of herself framed by lilies and gardenias and the picture she, Diane, had painted to Lloyd of a practical, energetic, keen girl just dying to get to work on the accounts when she wasn't packing moss and answering the telephone.

"Oh, I will, I will. When can I start?"

"Why don't you give him a call in the morning. I, er, don't suppose he'll be able to pay you a lot to start with. I mean, it's a sort of apprenticeship deal and, of course, you don't have a work permit."

"I'll apply for one right away. I'll work hard and soon I'll be utterly indispensable. I'd better go and get dressed now. I'm dreadfully late."

Sandy was always dreadfully late. The less she had to do the later she seemed to be. Always abjectly apologetic but late. Diane edged over to block Sandy's access to the bathroom. The bath sounded as though it was about to overflow, so she'd better get to the point quickly.

"There's another thing. Claire has a friend coming to town this weekend and she's asked him to stay here. That was before we knew you were coming, of course."

"Oh."

"But Nancy and Betty are looking for a third girl to share the rent at their place. It's small but not too expensive. Maybe if I

34

loaned you two hundred dollars, you know, to get started . . . ?"

"I'll pay you back out of my first paycheck. I think perhaps I'll move to a hotel, though, until I find a place of my own. That apartment of Nancy's is very dark, and it's in such a depressing neighborhood."

Before Diane had a chance to explain roughly what two hundred dollars represented in buying power and rent, the door-bell rang.

"New York can be very expensive . . ." she started weakly.

"Yes, isn't it? Oh, that must be Richard. Be an angel and give him a drink. Tell him I'll be ten minutes. Must dash now or I'll really be late."

The apartment seemed oddly quiet and bare without Sandy. Diane felt like a waif in a gothic novel, rattling around in a deserted castle. Or like Julie Christie, in *Darling*, alone in the palace in Italy, having made some irrevocable life mistake. Diane missed Sandy, the more so since Claire was held over in Rome for two extra days.

Diane missed Claire too. She missed her humor and her in-fluence. She had an element of wildness in her. Diane was now not alone in drunkenness and messiness, but a line was drawn. She could go as far as Claire did, which should be far enough for anyone, but no further.

Claire came back from Italy in good spirits, pleased to find Sandy evicted, and looking forward to seeing Ted. As far as Diane could make out, Claire's enthusiasm for her weekend with Ted had in no way cramped her style in Rome.

Diane did her best to keep away from the apartment during Ted's visit. She wanted to spare him the awkward necessity of inviting her to join them for meals and outings. But when Sandy called and suggested a dinner together, Diane's reaction was

35

much more than relief at a legitimate way of keeping out from under Claire's feet. She'd really missed Sandy.

Diane arrived at the restaurant half an hour late in a state of happy anticipation.

"Sorry I'm late. Philip always seems to have a crisis on Friday nights."

"That's what happens when you work for an artist," her date, Kenny, said, not looking as though he'd been doing any very serious pining. Sandy seemed happy enough too, and prettier than ever.

"You look terrific," Diane said to Sandy, being generous to compensate for her slight feeling of annoyance, something almost, but not quite, jealousy. "That's a lovely shirt. Have I seen it before?"

"No, I saw it this afternoon and fell in love with it. Frightfully expensive, but I think it's worth it."

Yes. Diane appraised the shirt quickly. That was where the two hundred dollars for rent had gone. Terrific. Lending—no, don't let's be euphemistic—giving Sandy that money had left her short for her own rent. She would probably have to borrow from Claire to pay her share. And it had been months since she'd bought any new clothes. And on top of that, now how was Sandy going to pay her rent? Well, after this she felt as adamant as Claire about not letting her back into the apartment. Let her pig it at the Y.W.C.A.

On the other hand, she couldn't forget the pearls. Not a great rope of pearls, but a string of pretty Victorian seed pearls. It made her more confused than ever. Just before Sandy left, and without any apparent forethought, she had taken the pearls off her neck and given them to Diane.

"This is for you. Thanks for everything."

"It's beautiful." And it was. "But it's yours. I couldn't possibly. For a start it's much too valuable."

36

It was obviously worth something and presumably of sentimental value to Sandy since she had never seen her without them. And the gesture was so obviously an impulse that Diane was afraid Sandy would regret it later.

"Please take it. I want you to have it. Please."

So Diane took it, hugged Sandy, and felt guiltier than ever about ejecting her.

And now Diane was wearing the necklace. And trying to rationalize her feelings. In fact, in terms of cold cash, the pearls were worth more than the total of rent, food, electricity and Vitabath consumed by Sandy. And the two-hundred-dollar loan. But, nevertheless, it was totally irresponsible, and since Diane wasn't about to pawn a present, the monetary value was irrelevant. It did nothing to help Diane's immediate balance of payments. And, though it was enormously generous to take a piece of family jewelry off one's neck and give it to a friend, it was wrong in some way. She looked at Sandy carefully. Something was missing, but she didn't understand exactly what it was. It was almost as if Sandy didn't understand that most actions had consequences. A disregard for the realities of life. Cause and effect.

"Sandy's been telling me about this creep she's been working for."

"I mean I'm not exactly afraid of hard work" (hard to contradict that one, Diane had never seen her face to face with it— possibly she was fearless), "but there's a limit. I mean this was sheer exploitation."

Poor Lloyd.

"Little fag obviously hates women." Kenny was usually no fool, so how come he was so completely taken in by Sandy? How come she, Diane, had never noticed his tendency toward sweeping psychological generalizations?

"He isn't a fag," she said, rather more sharply than she'd intended.

Thank God Claire wasn't there. She loved to say "I told you so." And she had told Diane. Not once and again, but again and again. "She doesn't want to be helped. She doesn't want a job, she doesn't want you to find her somewhere to live."

And now Sandy was making her sound like some recruiter for a sweatshop. Kenny was looking at her with disapproval. He was no prize, but still, Sandy should have kept her hands off. A poor thing, but her own. Her date.

Fortunately Sandy's own date returned before Diane showed herself in an even worse light. Richard was thin and threadbare and intelligent. Just Diane's type, the kind of man she'd enjoy spending time with. *Had* spent time with, in fact, since she used to chat with him while he waited for Sandy to finish dressing. Not the sort of man she'd have imagined waiting for any woman, or listening to Sandy's chatter without flinching. But he'd waited happily, patiently, and had taken her out time and again. Rather more grandly, Diane imagined, than he could afford.

"This is Dennis," Richard announced, seeming to feel this was an adequate introduction to the slightly overweight man who approached their table. Diane realized he'd forgotten Kenny's name, and maybe hers too. He was bored, and disappointed not to be spending the evening alone with Sandy.

She looked at Dennis. A weak face, she thought, but not unpleasant. Expensive clothes. Confidence. The headwaiter gave Dennis's chair a little shove as he quite slowly lowered himself onto it and she noticed that Sandy had perked up a little. Attention from headwaiters seemed to please her. The headwaiter hovered deferentially, and wished Dennis a pleasant evening, addressing him by name. Dennis thanked him, addressing him by name. He was known here. Sandy looked enchanted. Up to then the service had been nothing to write home about.

Diane looked Dennis over more carefully, trying to guess what he and Richard could possibly have in common. There was something not quite masculine about him, though without any suggestion of homosexuality. There was a short silence.

"Well," Dennis said, and seemed to find this an adequate icebreaker. Diane smiled nervously, but no one else seemed moved to keep the social ball rolling. Dennis considered them for a further moment. "What's everyone drinking?"

"Champagne," Richard said firmly.

"Champagne?" Diane echoed, startled, noticing Kenny's aghast expression. Up to then everyone had ordered with commendable modesty. "What're we celebrating?"

"Dennis paying."

Dennis laughed, but not as though he were very amused. Apparently the joke was too close to the truth. "Garçon," he called loudly, annoyed that the headwaiter had moved away to greet some new customers.

A waiter, not French, arrived to take their orders. Dennis asked for the wine list. There was another, rather more awkward silence. After a moment, Richard, either with a view to modifying his insult or bragging, now tendered an explanation.

"Actually, we're going to drink a toast to a new business venture."

"What venture?" Kenny asked, breaking a self-imposed silence.

"Dennis is going to produce my play."

"What play?" Sandy sounded interested, but not very.

"Something I've been working on for years."

"I didn't know you wrote plays," Diane said, nothing but admiration in her voice. Kenny was a corporation lawyer. How come Sandy was the one to get the only intellectual in the group? As if she didn't know.

"You don't know everything, my darling." Richard's voice was cold steel, and Diane realized the play, if it existed at all, was incomplete or in a very early stage. She tried to think how to change the subject quickly and still save face. She felt deeply hurt, and at the same time, embarrassed by her own tactlessness. But Sandy, for once, saved the day.

"Are you a theatrical producer?" she asked, all breathy. Her wide blue eyes looked at Dennis with respect and awe. Diane found herself wondering what his reply could be. She couldn't immediately imagine a suitable profession for Dennis. That he should actually produce plays seemed incredible.

"Not primarily. I'm in real estate. Property." Diane nodded, fortunately unnoticed by the others. Of course, the one business in which any shmuck born with a million could earn a buck. "But I have some investments which do include that field."

Dennis was pleased by Sandy's interest, and decided to order a more expensive brand of champagne than he'd originally planned.

Chapter Three

Ten days later, while Claire was serving almost completely defrosted scrambled eggs four thousand feet above Fort Lauderdale, and Diane was carefully measuring and mixing two brands of freshly roasted and ground coffee for Philip's ten o'clock tray, Sandy was sitting at a breakfast table in Westchester.

"Another cup of coffee, dear?"

"Mm." Sandy didn't look up from her copy of *Women's Wear Daily,* nor did Dennis's mother move a finger toward the coffee pot. She had timed her offer so that Mavis, white-uniformed and bearing more hot toast, could pour for both of them.

" 'The same little bird tells me that one of our favorite often-married stars is cheating on his ex-stewardess wife with a girl from another airline.' Now I wonder who that could be."

Sandy's eyes widened.

"Who do you think he is?" she asked.

"I don't know, honey, that covers a pretty broad range."

Sandy bit into another piece of toast, this one thickly spread with Little Scarlet preserves, and considered the question. Mom watched the passage of the toast from plate to mouth, tempted to have another piece herself. But it was a mistake to squander all one's calorie allowance for the day on one meal. She wanted to be able to enjoy herself at dinner, and if she was going to get into the pearl gray pyjamas . . . Never mind, the coffee was good, and cigarettes weren't fattening.

Dennis, who had eaten a hearty breakfast and disappeared with the *New York Times* for twenty minutes, returned, ready to go to the office. He kissed his mother on her forehead.

"Good-bye, Mom. Don't overdo it today."

"I won't, darling, and now I've got Sandy to look after me."

Both looked approvingly at Sandy. The epitome of well-bred, healthy English girlhood. Silky-haired, lightly made up and wearing a robe similar to, but newer than, the ones she had worn for breakfast with Diane.

Dennis crossed to the other side of the table and leaned over to kiss Sandy. She quickly swallowed her mouthful of toast, and raised her lips, almost absentmindedly. Mom beamed at the happy picture they made. A lovely couple. She thought perhaps Dennis was putting on a little weight. She'd wondered if he should have had that second muffin but, thank God, she wasn't one of those bossy or possessive mothers who interfered with their children's lives. And Dennis was her only son. She felt herself lucky he lived at home, and did her best to make things comfortable for him.

"Have a good day, darling. Don't work too hard."

Her eyes followed him as he left the room.

Diane got used to the change in Sandy's life style almost as quickly as Sandy did, which was instantaneously. Sandy had a knack, some might have called it almost a talent, for blending comfortably and pleasantly into any new surroundings. And giving pleasure to those around her. She filled in small but important gaps in Dennis and Mom's lives—as, in a way, she had in Diane's. Wife, daughter, sister. Diane missed her. More than she would have expected. She missed her gentle English voice, a contrast to the strident American ones she heard around her all day. She missed the pleasant attention to small domestic details, the food and flowers, the welcome home after a hard day and crowded subways.

Now they saw much less of each other. Sandy and Mom came into New York several times a week, and if Mom were busy and Diane were free, they lunched together. Usually when Philip was out of town or busy.

Sandy picked up the check each time, after protests from Diane. Not too strong protests. Sandy obviously wanted to return past hospitality and they lunched at places of her choice, well outside the range of Diane's budget. "I like to go where I'm known," was what Sandy said now. And echo of Dennis and probably of Mom, too. And where she was known, apparently, was Mortimers and trendy little, vaguely French restaurants on Madison.

But the largesse stopped at lunches. There was never an offer to repay the two hundred dollars. The money would have been useful, especially since Philip occasionally forgot to pay her on time, but Diane couldn't ask Sandy for it. Sandy signed the lunch checks with pride and a flourish, but Diane didn't know how she was fixed for actual cash. Maybe a request for repayment would force Sandy to ask Dennis for the money, which would be creepy. After a time she decided she had had two hundred dollars worth of lunches, not to mention the pearls, and she forgot about the money.

In fact, Sandy hadn't entirely forgotten the loan. She'd think, from time to time, "I really should repay Diane," but rather in the way another person might say: "I'd like to see the Himalayas before I die," or "I really should make the effort and get to Venice before it finally sinks into the water." No really pressing sense of urgency. Besides, she never had much cash about her.

Neither Mom nor Dennis ever pressed a note into her hand and said why don't you buy yourself whatever. Instead she could sign at certain restaurants. Mom signed or gave credit cards at Elizabeth Arden's and Saks. Actual cash seemed only to change hands with parking attendants and headwaiters. At the beginning Sandy muttered things like "I'll repay . . . er, Dennis will, of course," and so forth. But soon she learned to smile and say thank you. Maybe Dennis settled up with Mom, or for all she knew he paid the entire monthly accounts. No way of telling. He had, presumably, paid for the little red sports car which gave her such joy.

She realized Mom took pleasure in dressing her up, treating her like a new doll. And shopping for two added a new zest to Mom's busy days in the department stores. Lookalike dresses (more like sisters than mother and daughter, the assistant had said) for a small party they gave to announce, or rather not to announce but to hint at, Dennis and Sandy's engagement.

And it was important that people should know they were engaged, even if it was secretly. An engaged girl living, or better still, staying with the family of her betrothed had a good Edwardian, or gothic, ring to it. Beautiful, impoverished, upper-class English girl to marry rich, adoring young man. Why, Emily Brontë (or was it Charlotte?) could have done something with that. And, of course, Mom was a chaperon. What could be more respectable? Certainly nothing like being kept. More like the bridegroom's family buying the trousseau. Completely different. So what if she and Dennis shared a bedroom (a suite, actually, and that also seemed to make a difference) in Mom's house? This was the twentieth century, after all, and it would have been slightly suspect if they hadn't. Sandy never stopped to think that her slight defensiveness in this area was not to do with sex, but with the lack of it. For there wasn't very much. Which was okay, because sweet though Dennis was, she didn't really feel like that

44

about him. And after the first week of obligatory passion, she felt he was quite relieved to let the whole thing slide into an occasional bout of slightly clumsy lovemaking.

Sometimes it takes a strange collection of random events, all of which have to be synchronized, to cause another, quite separate event to take place. Diane might have worked for Philip for ten years without him ever taking her to bed, if several things hadn't conspired to get them there.

If Philip hadn't had lunch with his agent that day, for instance, it would never have happened. But he did, and though he was neither very interested in food and drink, nor in the habit of overindulging in either, he tended to increase his consumption when the Morris agency was footing the bill. It was some kind of subconscious getting his money's worth, not unlike the businessman who tries to eat and drink the difference in air fares between first and tourist. Billy, who struggled with a weight problem, and had a meeting at three o'clock with a notoriously fly-by-night producer who'd gotten the better of him in the past, sipped half a glass of wine. Philip finished the rest, and after lunch was feeling expansive enough to accept a small brandy. He went home in a more than usually good mood, flattered by Billy's attention, and virtuously secure in the knowledge that he'd done three pages of very good work that morning.

Even so, all might have been well if Diane had not been wearing a blue gingham dress. It was light and simple, and less sophisticated than what she usually wore to try to attract Philip's attention. She had no way of knowing that Philip had pined away his fifteenth year, painfully in puppy love with a girl who was now, unbeknownst to him, married to an undertaker. She'd gone for a sort of *Oklahoma*-like cuteness, which included plenty of bows and a fair amount of inevitable gingham. Philip had no interest in women's clothes, and for all he knew, or could remember, the girl of his adolescent dreams might have been dressed exclusively by Givenchy. But he did know that Diane reminded him of someone and that she suddenly looked very attractive.

Even so, he might have filed that faintly surprising reaction in the back of his mind and gone and had a two hour nap, if she hadn't been arranging flowers.

With Philip gone, and a new housekeeper installed, Diane had nothing to do. She'd retyped the pages he'd written and left them on his desk for the morning. There was hardly any mail and no lunch tray to prepare.

She'd decided to take apart the flower arrangement in the hall. Flowers, like windows, were apparently on the new housekeeper's list of untouchable objects. All morning, Diane had been aware that the water in the vase was low and stale and that several of the flowers were well past their best. Now, with an hour or two to spare, she'd spread out a newspaper on the kitchen table to keep peace with the housekeeper, who was putting her feet up in front of a soap opera. Diane had emptied all the flowers onto the kitchen table, thrown away the dead, and trimmed the ones which seemed to have a few more days of life. The vase was too large for the survivors so she scrubbed it and put it away. In the back of the cupboard she'd found a smaller vase which she'd never seen used in the house. It would do perfectly. She'd just finished the arrangement and was contemplating the results with pleasure when Philip returned. She'd done it very well, and had he been in a more perceptive frame of mind, he might have wondered why a girl with such a gift seemed to order stiff ugly flowers and plants for his girl friends.

"That's very pretty."

"I hope you don't mind. They'd really had it, and I think the daisies and this other stuff are good for a couple of more days. Where should I put it?"

"I think that vase used to go on the table in my room."

Diane picked up the vase and, followed by Philip, carried the flowers into his bedroom. He stood watching in the center of the room as she put the vase on a chest of drawers, in front of a mirror, and began to make a few minor alterations.

Philip was aware he hadn't seen a woman arrange flowers for years; his ex-wife was probably the last person to do it for him. Also the sending of flowers, by him, was a routine acknowledgment of sexual favors granted. Flowers, brought by a woman into his bedroom, had a definite erotic association. And Diane was looking prettier than ever in her cotton dress.

Diane, in the mirror, saw Philip approaching her, and managed to repress the urge to say something, anything, to break the silence. She was so aware of his presence, so attracted to him, that she was constantly afraid he must feel it.

"There. How's that, now?"

She took a half-step back to get a better look at her finished work. Philip placed one hand firmly on either side of her waist and squeezed.

"Very pretty. Like you."

For a moment their eyes met in the mirror. She saw his smiling, hers looking appalled and frightened, like a trapped rabbit. She lowered her look to the flowers, and even moved a trailing strand of creeper a couple of unnecessary inches to the left, playing for time, waiting for him to release her, or to give a clue as to the next move. She could feel her entire body stiffen, and knew he could feel her tension. She tried and almost succeeded in a small smile to let him know she knew it wasn't serious. To deny to him, and to herself, the overwhelming effect that just his hands on her fully clothed waist was having. It would be too humiliating if he guessed that this casual gesture was making it difficult for her to remember to breathe.

She should think of something light and funny to say, and then slip out of his grasp. But her mind was blank, and she continued to fiddle with the flowers, though her hands trembled slightly. After a moment, Philip slid his arms around her and pulled her back against him. Even though she knew this gesture could only be one of erotic invitation, she refused to believe it. Involuntarily, she raised her glance to meet his eyes in the mirror. But as his hand moved up to take one of her breasts her eyes closed and her body started to move against his.

Sandy moaned in sensuous pleasure. Her waist and hips moved slightly to relish the complete physical enjoyment of what was being done to her. Never had she felt so young, so firm, so tanned, so beautiful and admired. Her eyes were closed. If she hadn't been such a lady she might have allowed a small, soft moan to escape her lips. But she was, above all, a lady. Nevertheless, her back arched to feel the pressure of the masseuse's strong, firm, masterful hands.

For a moment her eyes opened and she saw Mom, limp and relaxed, covered with a light blanket and blinded by the pads on her eyes. She was helplessly struggling with cigarettes and a lighter, trying to smoke blindfolded.

Sandy closed her eyes again, gave herself up to the bliss of it all. Not only physical. The masseuse, while letting them know how discreet she was, also had indiscreetly let them know why her discretion was necessary. The names of her better known "regulars" had been mentioned. And they were the names Sandy and Mom read about in their gossip column and their magazines, saw almost daily photographed in *Women's Wear Daily*.

Sandy, turning over, reflected that she was twenty years younger than most of those women, and prettier. Her photograph would look well there. Maybe. Someday.

Philip had been asleep for half an hour, and Diane knew she should go home. There were women—Diane was not one of them—who would have napped or amused themselves until he woke up, and then have expected or maybe even demanded to be taken out to dinner. Of course, if Philip woke up in the next five minutes and suggested it, it would be heaven. But after five minutes she would go, so as not to look as though she were hanging around expecting something. Though a kiss or some small affectionate phrase would make everything perfect.

Diane had had a friend at Oxford, who'd been told by her doctor that she was pregnant and had, in the horror of the moment, cast logic aside and said: "But I can't be, I didn't even enjoy it." Diane thought of her and considered how unfair it was that, though she hadn't come, she was now seriously in love with Philip. And she imagined it wasn't a situation that would lead to happiness.

After fifteen minutes, and nothing more than a light snore from Philip, she slid out of bed, put on her clothes and, carrying her shoes, tiptoed out of the room.

Sandy looked approvingly at her own feet. Beautiful, unmarked and now tanned. Better not move them for another ten minutes, make sure the polish was completely dry. Anyway, there was no hurry. Mom was still under the dryer, leafing listlessly through *Psychology Today,* getting bored and fidgety, though she was not due to come out for another five minutes. Sandy looked around for something to distract her, and picked up a copy of *House and Garden*. Mom had already read it, it had been out for two weeks, but it was better than nothing.

"Look at that wonderful grandfather clock. Don't you think it's lovely?" she yelled, passing the magazine across.

"What's that?"

"The grandfather clock," Sandy shouted over the noise of the dryer. "Don't you love it?"

Mom smiled, nodded deafly, and took the magazine. As Sandy

had hoped, she admired the clock, then started to leaf through the other pages. Twelve-thirty. Sandy was hungry, though she'd had a late and substantial breakfast. She seemed to be eating more and more, and was looking forward to a leisurely lunch. She hoped Mom wasn't in one of her "quick salad, I've got to get to the linen department" moods. Sandy pressed a finger into her upper thigh. Yes, she was definitely putting on weight. The scales in her bathroom showed an increase of two pounds, so she'd better watch it. She could always exercise, she supposed, but recently she'd felt too tired. Dennis was the one who should exercise. Here she was, worrying about two pounds, and he needed to lose fifteen. He might make an effort. Surely he knew all that flab wasn't a very attractive sight.

She yawned, glanced at her watch. Think of something amusing to chat about at lunch, keep Mom in a good mood, then after coffee, maybe she could plead a headache, hint at the impending curse and go home and have a little nap.

A degree in English literature had not turned out to be everything Diane had been led to believe.

On the more obvious level, it had never got her a job that hadn't involved being able to type. Not that she'd thought of higher education as a passport to a well paid job, but still.

And at times when she could have used a little intellectual comfort, she tended instead to find, in fiction, disconcerting parallels to her own life. Like now. Somerset Maugham's housemaid story. What was her name? Never mind, the other parts of it were clear. There was this guy (he might even have been a writer) who had a maid, an absolute paragon. There was a scene in which he was angry with her because she'd taken all his books out to dust them, then he'd found they were all back in exactly the same order. He called her by her surname. Then for some reason, on her day off, he'd asked her to go to the movies with

50

him. They'd had dinner afterward, and then, almost by accident, he'd gone to bed with her. The next morning he woke up, appalled, realizing he'd now lost this marvelous servant. As he lay there cursing himself, she came in, uniformed as usual, bearing his breakfast tray and pretending nothing had happened the night before. As far as Diane could make out, he went on calling her by her surname.

The day after Diane had been to bed with Philip, she came to work feeling shy and awkward. Not quite knowing how to greet him, she waited to take a cue from him. None was forthcoming. She did not show in any way that she remembered the previous afternoon, and in a few minutes it was too late to say or do anything. The moment had passed.

For a few days, Diane retained the agonizing hope that they might repeat the experience, or that Philip would in some way acknowledge that they'd made love. By the weekend, she knew that neither was likely. And gradually she learned to live with it. There were a few bad moments, inevitable in a house with its layout, such as when she met a half-clad girl in the kitchen one morning, and the first time Philip asked her to order flowers for some new girl. But the second time these things happened, they didn't seem so symbolic and were a little, though not much, easier to deal with.

Sandy poured herself another glass of wine. She knew it was a mistake. It was fattening and made her sleepy, and she had a busy afternoon ahead of her. But she was bored and tired. This wasn't what she'd imagined decorating to be. She'd had an image of a good-looking, if not entirely macho young man listening, rapt and respectful, as she stood in the middle of an empty but beautiful room in her new house. She would be waving her arm around, throwing out ideas, a feeling of what she wanted. And it would all happen.

51

Instead it was tiring and her feet hurt. They had trudged through department stores, gone up and down in elevators, looked at hundreds of similar and unbeautiful things. The decorator was middle-aged, unattractive and superior. And he was talking to her, had apparently asked her a question, and seemed to be waiting for a reply.

" . . . carpet. What do you think?"

It was a token question. Sandy held no charms for him and he was irritated by her lack of enthusiasm. He was doing up a house for her, she was to a certain extent his client, but he was well aware that Dennis was paying the piper and Mom calling the tune.

"I don't know. You'd better ask Mom."

But Mom was deep in a conversation with her sister about employment agencies. Sylvia had come along because she enjoyed nothing so much as a nice day's shopping, and anyway she needed some new bedroom curtains and if they just happened to see something she liked, she knew the decorator wouldn't mind her using his number. Just this once. Mom was such a good customer.

The servant problem. Sandy remembered Diane had once told her the only two safe topics of conversation among adults, it had seemed to her as a small child in Ireland, were poultry and the servant problem. She supposed she should be grateful that here at least they didn't discuss chickens. She sighed. At moments like this she missed Diane, and her little apartment, and the cosy little chats they'd had over breakfast. The thing was to get this house finished, then she and Dennis would be married and move in. Lots of time then for little lunches with Diane, and the fun of having ordered that lunch, from her own staff, cooked in her own kitchen. Doing menus with the cook. Planning the flowers with the gardener. Intimate candlelight dinners for two. No, that

52

wasn't quite so pleasing as the daytime images. While Dennis was at work.

Sandy heard her name mentioned, and tuned in to real life. Mom was talking about her.

" . . . absolutely thrilled when Dennis told me he was bringing her home. 'Imagine it,' he said, 'twenty years old, an English rose, all alone in the world, and already holding her own among all those intellectuals and writers.' I just couldn't wait to meet her. I knew we were going to be friends from the start. Why, just the other day . . ."

And so on. Inevitably into the story of the salesgirl who'd allegedly thought them sisters. And it was all true; Mom had welcomed her with open arms, and no questions. She wished she'd forget the all-alone-in-the-world bit. Sandy'd never actually said she was an orphan. Mom had misunderstood and Sandy had never really corrected the mistake. She couldn't imagine her parents with Mom or Dennis, and had no plans to have them to the wedding. Mom and Dennis would seem very American and pretentious to them. And Sandy had managed to suggest she'd come from a long line of landed gentry, with a minor title or two in the background.

Her parents weren't dead. It was just that she'd put her family and that part of her life behind her. They were nothing to be ashamed of, but they wouldn't fit in to what her new life was to be. She'd grown out of them and moved on. Even before she came to America. She'd gone to London because she hadn't wanted to live in a small town in Kent. Where the best job available to her would be working in the office of the local estate agent. Where she would be expected to help her mother serve tea to groups of middle-aged church women. Where the pinnacle of the social season was the golf club dance. At the moment she might be bored, but she fitted in. These people recognized her real qualities. Who she really was. It was her parents who had gotten it wrong. She was beautiful, her taste was perfect, so were her manners. She could go all the way. And everything had a price. She understood that. And in her mind the price was not so much sharing a bed with Dennis but making everyone happy and keeping things pleasant. Even if it meant being bored and tired as she now was.

But soon it wouldn't matter; she would be married. Just as soon as Mom had steered them all through Christmas. Sandy would have liked to get married earlier, but she could see Mom's point of view. Christmas shopping and the buying of a trousseau were separate, should not be simultaneous. These things had to be done properly, and she was grateful no one wanted her to buy a wedding dress off the peg. Like the house, her dress would not be ready for a couple of months. It was all hard work and planning. In her way Mom put in a more strenuous day than Dennis did. And Sandy often returned home feeling tired and battered.

Sandy touched her ears, although she'd been told to try not to. Today she felt more than battered, she felt wounded. Her lobes were tender and suspiciously sticky. She hoped she wasn't bleeding onto her dress. Worse still, they were probably infected. No, they couldn't be, they'd only been pierced that morning. The temporary earrings were pure gold. Small, modest, but pure gold. "Just in case somebody gives you something pretty for Christmas," Mom had said coyly. And Sandy had allowed herself to be taken, pale and horrified, like an initiate to some pagan, disfiguring ritual. One of a series of physically painful and disgusting things women allowed to be done to their bodies, took for granted, even. Like childbirth, but then at least you ended up with a dear little baby, whereas . . . Actually, if she were given the earrings she had ingeniously admired, she supposed it was all worth it. But she still felt queasy and hadn't had the sympathy she'd expected. Mom had taken the whole barbaric ceremony in her stride. Even when the clumsy fool had pierced her lobes unevenly and the left one had had to be done over. Sandy had thought she would faint. She still didn't feel terrific. Perhaps she ought to have a small brandy.

Too late, Mom was calling for the check, was straining at the bit to return to the fabric department.

"What's wrong, sweetie?"

"Nothing. I'm just tired."

Dennis looked at Sandy with concern. She was lying on the bed, and her expression could only be described as sulky. She was pale, and Dennis had hopes that whatever was troubling her was only physical.

"I'm tired and I've got a headache and my feet hurt."

"Let me get you an aspirin. Would you like a drink?"

He brought her an aspirin from the medicine chest in the bathroom and a Tab from the tiny refrigerator in his dressing room. One of the little luxuries Mom had added to his suite, or apartment as she called it, to increase his feeling of independence. In theory, he could have friends up for a drink, or a girl to spend the night, without ever bumping into Mom in the downstairs bar. In practice the fridge went unused from month to month. Mom had one in her room, too, but only makeup and medicines were kept in it.

"Thank you, darling."

Sandy liked to be made a fuss of, and anyway it was important to have Dennis on her side. This would be a kind of test for the future.

"Why don't you try and take a little nap before dinner."

"No, I'll be all right. It's just that I had a ghastly day."

"What happened?"

"We must have walked ten miles. We spent the entire morning looking at linens. There were the most beautiful Porthault sheets, but Your Mother said they were too expensive. We must have spent the difference in shoe leather by the time we found some others. And not nearly so nice."

Dennis looked sympathetic, worried and evasive. All at the same time. Sandy had put him on the spot. What did she expect him to do? Run downstairs and tell Mom he and Sandy refused to sleep on Fieldcrest?

"I'll tell Mom not to wear you out like this, it's not good for you."

But he knew, and she knew he knew, that what Sandy was complaining about was not her tired feet. It was the first time either Mom or Dennis had refused her anything. Not that she ever asked for things, but what she admired she usually was given.

"Who's coming to dinner?" Dennis changed the subject, sitting down on the end of the bed and massaging Sandy's bare, recently bathed and moisturized feet.

"The Gilberts and Joe and Aunt Sylvia."

"What're you going to wear?"

Sandy glanced at her built-in cedar closet which ran the entire length of one wall, and shrugged.

"I don't know. What difference does it make? Sylvia will be wearing some of those Pucci pyjamas of hers and Lorna Gilbert always looks as though she buys her clothes in airport shops between planes."

Dennis looked uncomfortable. This sort of malice was useful when it was used to divert and amuse Mom, and he felt content listening to them gossip and criticize. But this wasn't being said for laughs, it was a complaint. She was bored, discontent. Maybe he should have a word with Mom about the Porthault sheets. They seemed to mean a lot.

"Um . . . Philip . . ."

"What? Yes?" He sounded distracted, preoccupied, his tone

designed to make Diane feel like the butcher's boy from Porlock. Diane knew him better than that, and would never have interrupted him if he'd really been working. But sulking was another matter. And there was nothing random about her timing. The moment had been carefully chosen, and a variety of openings rehearsed.

To Philip's chagrin and Diane's delight his girl of the moment had stood him up for Christmas. She'd had a better offer and was off to Acapulco for a week. Diane gave him twenty-four hours to get over his immediate bad temper. Then hit him with the invitation.

"I wondered . . . if you're not doing anything else . . . I've been asked to a Christmas party in Westchester and Claire and I wondered if you'd like to come with us. We could all drive out together."

Philip hesitated for a moment. And Diane quickly but subtly let him know the party would be quite grand. Good food and drink, no question of bringing a bottle.

After a moment, he said he'd like to come. He'd no other plans and Diane had obviously taken their ill-advised afternoon in her stride, would never presume on it. It was unlikely to be the party of the year, and Diane wouldn't be his first choice of date, but he had nothing else planned and the holidays were getting close. So, all right. Diane quite easily followed his thought processes, thought him a cold-blooded shit and was still happy when he said yes.

Claire wasn't much easier to deal with. When they were originally invited she allowed as wild horses wouldn't drag her to spend Christmas Eve with Sandy and her new family.

"Of course they wouldn't," Diane agreed. "But would champagne and a well cooked meal and maybe even a little token off the tree?"

Claire's resolution wavered for a moment, but she stood firm. Ted was away, though, and nothing exciting had come up. As the days passed, and it looked as though she would have to defrost and eat her turkey dinner alone, she ungraciously changed her mind.

Sandy was delighted; now she would have her two oldest friends in America there for her first Christmas. Diane was moved by this. Claire said if she was one of Sandy's oldest friends, the problem of what to give her was solved: A Dale Carnegie course was obviously called for. But her heart wasn't in it. She had a sneaking admiration for the way Sandy had landed on her feet. She neither approved of nor envied Sandy's new-found life style, but points were awarded to a penniless girl arriving in New York who had done so well for herself so fast. The highest words of praise Diane had ever heard from Claire were, "She's a survivor," and the most critical, far more damning than her imaginative obscenities, "She's so goddamn helpless." Claire had originally reckoned Sandy to be semihelpless or, perhaps more accurately, pseudohelpless, and now she had to be reclassified as a Grade A survivor.

It was almost like being married. Not in the honeymoon sense. Claire, silent, in the back seat. Philip, driving and bitching. Diane, trying to decipher a map in the dim light, a map which seemed to have left out most of the minor, forked roads. The forked roads themselves either unsignposted or bearing names neither shown on the map nor included in Sandy's vague directions. Diane was apologetic and heard herself sound like an inefficient secretary instead of Philip's date and co-victim.

She found her reaction to his carping magnified by Claire's silent presence. She was used to his ungraciousness, but was aware that Claire's reaction, had their roles been reversed, would have been different.

"We've only got half a tank of gas left," Philip said accusingly.

Diane stifled a reflex which would normally have produced an apology.

"We're sure to find a gas station in the village," she said.

"On Christmas Eve?" His tone critical and sarcastic.

Claire stopped whistling through her teeth for long enough to intone: "In the unlikely event that it should become necessary, emergency exits are located in the forward and aft of the cabin, and life jackets. . . ."

"Christmas comes but once a year," Mom said, popping a fois gras canapé into her mouth.

No one contradicted her. Dennis took it, quite rightly, as encouragement to sample another crispy square of toast piled with caviar as he refilled their glasses with icy cold champagne.

There was a moratorium on all diets until after the New Year. January was the month when Mom put in her pre-spring two-week stint at the Golden Door, so what was the point of starving herself now? The goose, turkeys and ham now cooking in the kitchen, all their trappings, the Christmas pudding with hard sauce and mince pies to follow, had not in any way affected the quantity or quality of the hors d'oeuvres Mom's neatly uniformed maids passed around with pre-dinner drinks. Finger food, she called it. And prided herself on its variety, beauty and her total lack of economy. Lorna Gilbert might think that her cocktail guests either did not care or couldn't tell the difference between Beluga and lumpfish roe, but at Mom's house one was in no danger of such frugality.

Sandy was an invaluable asset on this occasion. She made it an excuse for Mom to produce a full scale, no holds barred, English Christmas party. And her clever ideas had supplemented Mom's already considerable range of hors d'oeuvres. In fact, the salver, covered with hollowed out cucumber stuffed with a sort of hot crabmeat filling, had been her idea.

59

Mom moved a carved radish to the exact center of the tray and glanced at her new watch. Ten minutes until their guests should arrive.

Diane had never seen Sandy look more beautiful. Radiant was what she was, but Diane would have been taking her life in her hands if she'd used that word in front of Claire.

"Pretend we've just met and you think I'm fascinating." Claire arrived at Diane's elbow. "I don't know a soul here and now that I've met one or two of the guests, I'm planning to keep it that way. Do you think she'd put my dinner in a doggy bag and let me call a cab?"

"Come on, give them a chance. Maybe Somebody Wonderful will come with the B group after dinner."

But Diane did not feel any more comfortable than Claire. Certainly less physically comfortable. The dress she'd borrowed from Claire that had looked so glamorous in their apartment looked ordinary beside the more expensive competition. And it felt too tight under the arms. She was unpleasantly aware she was beginning to sweat into it. The room was very hot. As far as Mom was concerned, you couldn't have an English Christmas without lots of holly and a big log fire. That didn't necessarily mean you had to turn the thermostat down. Diane, who'd been brought up in a big drafty house, had never got used to American heating. A Christmas party in Ireland meant women in evening dresses huddled around a fireplace, keeping themselves warm with whiskey as most of the heat went up the chimney. There was an ever present threat of chilblains.

Socially she felt more uncomfortable than Claire did. She didn't really care very much what kind of impression she made on Mom or Dennis. But she desperately wanted Philip to see her in a favorable light. Which didn't mean chatting animatedly to her roommate. This was the first evening she'd ever spent with

Philip, and she couldn't foresee the opportunity of another one. Ever since the afternoon he'd taken her to bed, Diane had been more and more painfully in love with him, and more and more desperate not to show it. She knew if he had any idea how strong her feelings were, he'd find an excuse to fire her, however hard it might be for him to find a replacement who did what she did for the same money. So she'd become crisper, impersonal, even more efficient, and after a week or two he'd become reassured. Probably even thought she'd forgotten the whole incident. Then had come the invitation to the Christmas party, and Sandy's casual suggestion that Diane bring a date if she wanted. Diane had leaped at the chance. Obviously any evening she might spend with Philip could only come about through her instigation. He'd never invited her, and though she'd often rehearsed privately, silently, a casual invitation to drop in on his way to . . . come and have a bite after . . . she couldn't quite imagine him in their pokey little apartment, eating a home-cooked meal on the kitchen table, or with a plate balanced on his knees in front of the television. Even if Claire sportingly disappeared for the evening. Another difference between her and Sandy. Were their roles reversed, by now Sandy would have lucked into house-sitting some elegant apartment on Park, and would entertain the man of her choice to baby lamp chops wearing little paper panties and all the garnishes. The meal would look like an illustration from *House and Garden*, and the flowers and fruit would be minor still lifes in their own right. To be fair, though, were she living in Diane's apartment, she'd probably have bought some inexpensive pillows for the floor, hung the walls with batik and entertained her guests to paella. Diane just didn't have her touch. Food had always been in some way awkward. The limited meals that could be cooked over a single gas ring in her bed-sit at Oxford, with the accompanying problems of food smells and an unsympathetic landlady weren't conducive to entertaining. To say nothing of an inadequate table, one chair and a single bed. And at home. In Ireland. Her mother had solved, or opted out of the menu problem. Roast beef on Sunday, cold on Monday, shepherd's pie on Tuesday. And so on. Defeated by depression and the impossibility of convincing the inexpensive local cook that cabbage could be fully cooked in less than an hour and a half. Again the accompanying smells hadn't been encouraging.

But this evening might be different. Since she and Philip were on neutral ground, since it was clearly some kind of exception to the rest of their life, maybe he would take her home to bed afterward. Just one more time.

She watched Philip's progress around the room. Mom was introducing him to Sandy. Diane looked at Sandy's backless black dress which emphasized her glowing skin and her new diamond earrings, and sighed. She glanced at a holly-encrusted mirror and noticed that her hair was beginning to lose its set.

Mom was pleased to see Sandy talking so animatedly to one of her guests. Although Sandy was beautiful and happy and chatty tonight, there'd recently been other occasions when she'd been little more than polite. Silent, withdrawn, not the sparkling, gay girl she'd been when she arrived. There had been that evening when she'd barely answered when Lorna Gilbert had spoken to her, and had stifled a yawn in the middle of one of Sylvia's stories. Maybe once Sandy and Dennis were married, she, Mom, should concentrate on a younger set. Dennis had always seemed content to mingle with her contemporaries, but now that she was about to add Philip to her A list, maybe she would go for a more exciting type of party.

And Mom just adored Philip. After five minutes exposure to his charm, she began to plan a new kind of party. A small intimate dinner with a lot of good conversation. Less formal than the ones she normally gave. She would be almost silent, a good listener, but occasionally leading the good-looking, well-dressed intellectuals, who would be her guests, into a new topic. She would become known for her salon. There would be witty conversation and discussion of books and the theater. How lucky that Diane had brought him. She must tell Sandy to invite Diane to have lunch with them one day next week. All girls together. She probably wouldn't ask Diane to the first of the new dinners; it wasn't as though she and Philip were "together" or anything. He'd made it very clear, in a subtle way, that he was just her boss and their being out together this one evening was not part of a pattern.

She led Philip over to meet Sylvia. About two minutes there and then on. Just enough to whet Sylvia's appetite—she couldn't afford to allow Philip to settle in one place for too long. He'd arrived late and dinner was in ten minutes. There were others to be impressed. Lorna Gilbert, for instance, though their rivalry was friendly and usually stopped at oneupmanship in the area of table linen. She'd allow Lorna about a minute and a half before she brought Dennis over to be introduced. Just in case Lorna couldn't work out the ground rules. Philip was Mom's catch; an invitation to Lorna's house was definitely not on. Lorna was even more impressed than Silvia, and Mom felt a little glow as she glanced around at her almost-daughter-in-law, her sister and her best friend, and thought how happy she was making them. Poor Lorna was quite overcome, desperately impressed by Philip and painfully aware that, thought she knew he was a famous writer, she couldn't actually remember the title of even one of his books. Mom reminded herself that tomorrow she must drop in at her local bookstore and order all his books. Perhaps she would ask him to autograph them for her. Or would that appear naive?

Diane felt a little better. Philip was with her and he seemed to be having a good time. She managed to suppress a feeling of disapproval that he should be so susceptible to the charms of Mom's middle-class affluence. Surely she wouldn't have wanted him to be awkward or reserved. What she did want, she supposed, was to have him by her side. Together, superior and amused by the company, while enjoying the benefits of Mom's hospitality.

"Listen, I'm going to get quietly plastered. Don't worry, I won't take my clothes off or tell dirty stories. But liquor is called for," Claire said.

"All right, bring me one, too."

Maybe a second drink would give her a little boost, a lift that would help her to circulate, chat up the other guests, appear relaxed and confident in front of Philip. Her eye kept going back to where he sat on the sofa, talking to Sandy. Both he and Sandy, it seemed, had taken advantage of Mom's last-minute instructions to her staff and were sitting on a sofa by the fire. Behind them now stood Claire, openly eavesdropping, leaning over so far that they were in imminent danger from the two full glasses she held. She caught Diane's disapproving look, shook her head and let her eyes roll back.

"Now I've heard everything," she said on her return.

"What?"

"Do you know what that pretentious creep—sorry, your *date*—is talking to Miss Birdbrain about? He's going to make her a book list, and she's so thrilled and wide-eyed."

Diane felt the familiar irrational pang she always did when men she expected to be above Sandy's charms succumbed to them.

Sandy wished they'd all go away. That is, all except Philip. In a moment or two Mom would come back from the kitchen and sweep them all off to the Christmas tree. Couldn't they leave her in peace for five minutes to have the first intelligent conversation she'd ever heard in this house? But Sylvia, or Aunt Sylvia as she urged Sandy to call her, was bearing down on one side. On the other, Claire was perched on the arm of the sofa, wearing the expression she sometimes had in the past when she thought Sandy was getting more than her fair share of attention from someone else's man. As though she thought Sandy was flirting with Philip. Which just went to show what a low mind Claire had.

She looked away from her hurriedly, and caught Lorna Gilbert also making the most of Mom's absence.

"I don't know much about books," she was saying, sliding onto the sofa, "but I do enjoy a good read."

"Just like me." Sandy flinched, anticipating Claire's customary sarcasm. "Who'd ever have thought we'd have so much in common. Do you know, I'll bet she knows nothing about art, but knows what she likes."

"Shh." She heard Diane hiss, presumably on the principle that if they could hear Lorna, Lorna could hear Claire's much louder voice.

Sandy felt a momentary pang of guilt about Diane, who didn't seem to be having a very good time. She supposed she really should have spent more time talking to her, doing her duty as a hostess, but there were so many other people to look after. So many other people, and they all seemed to be sitting on her sofa, butting in to her conversation. If they'd all go away she'd deal with them all separately later. And charm them all, with the possible exception of Claire. But later.

First of all she should rescue Philip from Lorna. He seemed stuck for an appropriate reply to the "good read" statement or confession, and had settled for a smile as though he'd been complimented. Lorna rattled on, asking him if he'd enjoyed *Shogun* as much as she had. And, worse still, Mom was bearing down on them with Dennis in tow.

"Philip, I'd like you to meet my son, Dennis, who's about to make this little girl my daughter. As I'm sure she's been telling you."

Dennis opened his mouth to let some cliché escape and Sandy, for the first time, felt embarrassed. Up to now she'd been proud of her affluent surroundings, of being engaged, of being just a couple of months away from becoming a prominent, fashionable young hostess. Admittedly, Richard had been unpleasantly sarcastic when she'd told him she wouldn't be able to see him again, but he was just jealous. Now her comfortable surroundings seemed just the littlest bit vulgar. Rich and good-natured were Mom's and Dennis's most prominent attributes and she suddenly wished she could, without being disloyal, show Philip she was better born than they were. She decided that when they were married, without being unkind to Mom, she and Dennis would have a separate group of friends they saw from time to time. She'd continue Mom and Sylvia and Lorna and the rest of them in a sort of family situation, but there'd have to be dinner parties and gatherings to which they weren't invited. As a young bride she would be a hostess in her own right, not an offshoot of Mom. Of course, Dennis would have to be handled carefully, tactfully, but if she invited a couple of people he did business with he'd be perfectly happy talking to them and it would, not to put too fine a point on it, keep him out of her way while she ran the more important side of it. Surely that should be possible. Mom didn't own him. Or maybe she did. For the first time the awful thought struck Sandy that perhaps Mom held the purse strings; maybe she put subtle pressure on Dennis to keep him at home. In that case Sandy would have to go more carefully. And she should find out. Casually. An occasional question to Mom when Dennis wasn't there. And vice versa.

She caught Philip's eye and with a small smile tried to disassociate herself from her new family before Dennis gave them his usual five minutes on how he didn't have time to read, with the definite implication he had better and certainly more important things to do.

Fortunately, at this moment the carol singers arrived.

Not everyone greeted their imminent performance with the same enthusiasm.

"Carol singers. You never told me there'd be carol singers," Claire accused Diane.

"I didn't know. You don't have to sing. It's not so terrible."

"Not so terrible. That depends what scale you're using. If a broken nail scores one point and inoperable brain cancer hits the jackpot with a hundred, carol singers start with a guaranteed sixty-five and in these surroundings I'd give them, oh, let's be conservative, ninety-three. That's without any added attractions like, for instance, little Pollyanna here getting up and doing a solo."

But the idea of carol singers, the surprise element, was the main attraction for Mom, and after a carol or two they were encouraged to take off their woolly hats and mufflers and have some mulled wine. They had served their purpose and now it was time to unwrap the presents. Or at least some of the presents. Tomorrow morning there would be the stockings to be unpacked, later tonight the more pedestrian gifts under the tree. But now was the perfect moment for a captive audience. Leaving the ceremony until midnight or even after dinner was dangerous, people had been known to slip away, and those remaining were bloated and their ability for enthusiastic response dulled by the enormous quantities of heavy starchy food mandatory at such a meal.

Sandy was the principal unwrapper. Love Dennis as much as she did, Mom understood that her little boy, unwrapping his

67

goodies, silk ties and cuff links, was a sight best appreciated by her and Sandy. But Sandy, pink with pleasure, tearing open surprise after surprise, was another matter. There was the Cinderella aspect of it for drama, and Sandy's first Christmas away from home was the excuse. But for Mom she might never have had this absolutely professional and complete set of photographic equipment. For her new career.

"Her new what?" Claire croaked.

"You heard her." Diane was no longer defending Sandy.

"You need all that stuff to shop? I thought a complete set of charge plates did the trick."

"As a special, you know," Sandy was burbling on. "On movies. Two or three days on the set. For magazines, *Time* and *Newsweek* and what's the other one?" Sandy felt the need to stress her imminent career, to show herself as a serious person. It would make up for some of the frivolity and vulgarity around her. She managed to tune out Claire's loud question about the location of the nearest john to throw up in.

Diane edged away from Claire—there'd be no stopping her now—and edged toward Philip. Now that he was no longer the center of attention, it would be a good time to have a moment with him. If she could think of something to say.

The photography equipment was stacked away on one side, Sandy's earrings were admired, and Mom was ready for the next thing.

"We'll eat in about ten minutes. Come on, Sandy dear, we must circulate."

And Sandy was led off to meet Cousin Frances. Fortunately, after a moment, Mom was called off to another group, and Sandy was free to plead the necessity of a last-minute check in the dining room, thereby making her escape and at the same time scoring points as a hostess. She crossed the hall, with no more than a short curious glance at the remaining stack of presents with her name on them.

In the dining room she walked slowly around the table, checking the place cards. By simply changing her card with Diane's, she put herself next to Philip. With any luck, Mom might think the mistake had been her own.

Chapter Four

"Sure. She's here. Hang on a minute."

Claire, one hand inadequately covering the mouthpiece, shouted: "Diane, it's for you. Your friend from the big house on the right side of the tracks."

It was now early February, and it seemed there was, at least in Claire's mind, no statute of limitations on Diane's responsibility for Sandy in general, and the Christmas party in particular.

Diane took the telephone, and was sorry to see Claire settle down a couple of feet away. Diane enjoyed a good girlish gossip with Sandy, and was going to be inhibited by Claire's asides.

"Guess what?" It had to be something major from the self-congratulation in Sandy's voice.

"What?"

"I'm married."

"You are? How wonderful, but I thought the wedding was next month."

"We got married at City Hall. This morning."

"Congratulations." But how odd. Could Sandy be pregnant? It seemed the only possible explanation. "And much happiness."

"Aren't you going to ask who to?" Sandy was really enjoying herself.

"What do you mean?"

"Don't you want to know who I married?"

"You mean . . . ?

"Yes."

"But . . . weren't you . . . surely . . ."

"Philip."

"Philip?"

Claire, who had, in fact, been more interested in the copy of *Vogue* on her knee than in the telephone conversation, looked up. The cold, tight despair in Diane's voice got her attention.

"Yes."

Claire watched, transfixed, helpless and full of pity. Diane had regained control of her voice, and now sounded surprised but amused and pleased. But Sandy couldn't see her face: white and stiff with pain, her eyes closed, oblivious to Claire. All her concentration going on maintaining control for Sandy.

"Yes. Isn't it wonderful? I'm so happy. And now think how much you and I'll be seeing of each other."

"Right." Her head sagged forward. Claire thought, for a moment, Diane was going to faint. But she reached out and clawed around for a cigarette. Claire got up, put a cigarette in her mouth, lit it for her. Diane's hands were too shaky even to get the matches open.

"So you should be flattered I'm interrupting my honeymoon to give you the good news. Though to tell the truth I need a little rest."

Claire, in the kitchen, poured a stiff brandy for Diane, then one for herself. She might have known. She did know, really, that Diane was a little in love with Philip, but she so disapproved of it she tended to laugh it off, imagining Diane could be ridiculed out of it. But this was something else. She went back into the room where Diane was now off the telephone.

"Thought you'd need this. I do. Even the shortest conversation with Birdbrain turns me toward the nearest bottle."

Diane took the drink gratefully. Grateful not only for the first burning gulp of brandy, but for Claire pretending she hadn't noticed.

"I take it Sandy's landed another live one?"

Diane nodded, managed a weak smile.

"And you hadn't a clue?"

A shake of the head; Diane still couldn't speak.

"A marriage made in heaven. I can't think of two people who deserve each other more. That sneaky little bitch and that cheap pompous . . ."

"Please don't . . ."

"I'm sorry. Please don't cry . . ." And Diane found herself in Claire's arms sobbing uncontrollably, soaking the shoulder of Claire's best white silk shirt with an indelible mixture of salt tears and mascara.

"He's not really like that . . ."

Claire thought it best not to express her amazement that Diane should choose to defend Philip at a moment such as this.

"Listen, I judge him by one standard only. Does he make you happy. If you came through the door with Attila the Hun on one arm and a happy smile on your face, I'd treat him like a brother and offer him some duty-free champagne. But Philip has done nothing but make you miserable, so in my book he's a bastard."

Fifteen minutes later Diane was tucked into bed, washing down two Valium with a mug of brandy-laced hot milk. Over her feet an extra blanket attractively decorated with the name of an airline. Claire went to try to salvage her blouse with Woolite and Diane was left to her thoughts.

72

Now certain things were falling into place. There'd been a new girl in Philip's life. At first Diane hadn't noticed it wasn't still the actress who'd stood him up at Christmas. Hadn't noticed. One way of putting it. Diane went to extreme lengths not to notice. Kept out of the way in the mornings until even the laziest girl would have awakened and taken herself off the premises. And recently there had been fewer confrontations. Almost as though the girl, whoever she was, didn't want to be seen. This sometimes happened. Married women in the afternoons mainly. But once Diane had gone into the room adjoining Philip's bedroom, looking for a missing page of manuscript, and had seen the door closing hastily. And there had been a familiar sound, a sort of *click-click-click*. Now, suddenly, she could place that sound. Sandy's bracelets. Sandy had three matching ivory bracelets; every time she raised or lowered her arm they clicked together. Well, well, well.

"Are you sure you wouldn't be happier in another line of work? A job in the sewers? Become New York's first garbage-person?" Claire asked, lighting another cigarette.

"Probably. But I don't know how to quit without looking sulky. I can't very well say: 'You married my friend and I'm jealous and I don't want to work for you anymore.' If I came up with a better offer, that would be an acceptable excuse, but I haven't."

"Shouldn't be hard to match for pay and conditions. I suppose it's no good trying to persuade you to join the ranks of dedicated young women whose spirit, courage and unfailing promiscuity ease the lot of the weary businessman on his way home to Denver?"

"I get airsick."

"You should think about it, all the same. You could meet twenty men just as shitty as Philip every week. And think of the stuff you could rip off."

"I don't like drinking out of miniature bottles. It makes me feel like Alice in Wonderland."

"Do you want me to come with you?"

Diane, startled, looked at Claire. She was wearing an old bathrobe and hadn't brushed her hair, and was chain-smoking sympathetically over Diane's untouched breakfast. For the first time since Sandy's bombshell, Diane laughed.

"No, Monday mornings are grim enough, anyway. But thanks."

Letting herself in Philip's front door, Diane almost wished she'd taken Claire up on her offer. She felt like an intruder, as though she were tastelessly forcing herself on them. But Philip had not suggested her taking a day off. In fact, as Claire often pointed out, Diane worked many more days a year than the average secretary. Memorial Day and the various presidents' birthdays meant nothing to Philip.

Well, now she was in the front hall. The house was silent and there was no sign of life. Diane, uncomfortably aware the honeymooners were probably still in bed, decided to follow the daily routine as best she could. She went into the kitchen, and started a pot of coffee, remembering to make one third more than usual. The kitchen was cleaner and tidier than it often was on a Monday. No signs of cooking, but an empty champagne bottle in the garbage. They must have eaten out.

Diane picked up the mail in the hall and tiptoed, she wasn't quite sure why, to the office. She felt a little calmer once she was at her desk. For some reason it would have been worse bumping into either of them in the hall or on the stairs. She wasn't sure which one she dreaded meeting most. Probably Philip. With Sandy she knew what her reaction was supposed to be. Kissing, laughing, congratulations. With Philip it would be harder. He had to be aware he'd behaved poorly toward her, even if he didn't know the full extent of her infatuation.

Naturally, Philip was the one she had to deal with first. Diane could see immediately the line he was going to take. He was matter-of-fact, accepting her congratulations calmly and moving on to the next subject. Rather as though she were a distant acquaintance and he was in a hurry.

Fine, she could easily follow that lead. If he wanted to be matter-of-fact, his performance was going to play a poor second to hers. She put the mail in front of him, returned to her desk and picked up her pencil and notebook. She couldn't help being pleased to see him somewhat nonplussed by this. He started to glance through his mail. Diane opened a folder on her desk, and found a letter she'd kept back from the mail on Friday. Philip meticulously answered fan mail, but usually dictated his replies. Occasionally, when the letter came from someone very grand he would reply with a handwritten letter. Diane spelled perfectly, and Philip had trouble getting cat right on the first try. She usually pointed out any errors tactfully, often referring to them as a "slip of the pen." Now she neatly folded a letter to a *New York Review of Books* critic which contained two gross spelling mistakes, sealed the envelope and put it in her out tray.

Philip cleared his throat; she looked up. He was smiling at her.

"I think we might begin with this one. Let me read you how it starts: 'As a working free-lance writer, you are undoubtedly seeking reliable information and practical advice on *how to write* publishable material and *where to sell it.*' And so on and so forth. And then a list of the prominent writers who contribute—a drearier line-up of tired old hacks you'd have trouble finding anywhere. Fortunately they've been thoughtful enough to enclose a postage-paid, self-addressed envelope. So I don't think we should waste the opportunity."

He started to dictate the letter. It was funny and clever and sarcastic, and Diane laughed several times. She was aware that Philip was composing this letter for her entertainment as much as his own. He wanted to keep her on his side, to keep her loyal to him, and above all to prevent her ever feeling moved to confide in Sandy any details of their afternoon together.

Claire looked approvingly at Diane. She'd been away for three days. In fact, since the morning she'd offered to accompany Diane to work. Diane didn't seem exactly happy, but Claire was ready to settle for the absence of either swollen eyes or a red nose.

And she had good news.

"I may have gotten you a job."

"Thanks, Claire, but the airlines are second only to the CIA when it comes to reluctance to employ illegal aliens."

"No, I don't mean a flying job. That was just a joke. It's fine for me, but I don't think you're really cut out for it."

Diane raised her eyebrows in mock umbrage.

"No, listen. There was this guy in First. He'd had quite a lot to drink and he asked me for my number. You'll be amazed to hear I didn't give it to him."

Diane nodded, not really amazed. Claire's standards in lovers were low, but unshakable.

"So he gave me his card, which said he was a movie producer and asked me if I wanted to get into movies. I explained that flying was a vocation for me, but I had a friend who was looking for a job. So he said why don't you give him a call."

"Thanks, Claire. You're a real pal. What ever would I do without you?"

"Well," Claire said, trying not to sound defensive, "it's worth a try. What have you got to lose? Tell you what," she continued, lifting the telephone and dialing the number on the card she'd been trying to press on Diane. "I'll just give Mitch a call right now. If I leave it to you, you'll go all British and shy on me, and never do it."

76

"Mitch," echoed Diane in aghast tones, as though his name alone confirmed all her earlier suspicions.

"Mitch," reechoed Claire, nothing but confidence in her voice. "It's Claire. . . . Claire. I'm the one you met on the plane. . . . You know, the pretty one, blond hair and big boobs? . . . Right?"

Diane listened aghast as Claire made an appointment for her the following day.

"There you are," she said. "Now if you'll stop looking so glum I'll cook dinner."

"You will? What?"

"Oh, the usual. One of my specialties. Tender chunks of filet de boeuf oh jew, smothered with hand-fed tomatoes, fresh baby petit pois and served with succulent dwarf potatoes from New Jersey's heartland."

"You're going to heat up the leftover stew?"

"There you go, as we say in the sky. And to drink? May I suggest some château bottled, rare vintage Gallo?"

Sandy, as healthy, happy and energetic as a young cocker spaniel, and with about the same attention span, greeted Diane.

"You poor darling, you must be exhausted with all those groceries. I'd give you a hand, but I've got to keep kneading this dough for another four mintues."

Diane carefully lowered her load onto the kitchen table, her arms aching. Nevertheless, her primary emotion was one of gratitude. Gratitude Claire wasn't there. Claire might be her closest friend, but a large part of Diane's working day was spent celebrating her absence. Her absence at this particular moment was on a series of European flights that read like the Grand Tour. Not that any of it would rub off on Claire. She would eat at McDonald's in Paris, drop a coin in the jukebox at Salzburg,

77

send a Mickey Mouse postcard from Florence and, time permitting, take in the new James Bond movie at Stratford-on-Avon.

Her parting words had been: "Okay, you can keep on working for Scott until I fix you up with another job. But if I come back and find Zelda has you rinsing out her undies I'll march right in there and take you away."

It hadn't quite come down to laundry. Yet. Although Sandy, happy and generous, tried to include Diane in the honeymoon spirit of the house, she had also begun to say things like, "Darling, could you possibly . . . Would you mind terribly . . . Sweetie, while you're out, could you just collect . . ." There was also a fair amount of additional work involved in Sandy's minor redecorating schemes although these were fizzling out. At the beginning, perhaps because she had been cheated out of a full-scale decorator house, or because she wanted to put her personal mark on a house Philip had lived in for five years before he met her, Sandy had had grand ideas about doing the place over. But Philip wasn't interested in spending money, and Sandy was basically lazy and had had enough shopping in the last few months to hold her for some time.

"Would you be an angel and stuff those things in the fridge? I daren't stop now or it'll all be spoiled."

Diane looked at Sandy with grudging admiration. Married two weeks and looking like the glowing bride out of a bad television Western. Crisp blue gingham dress, and her smooth blond hair in pigtails. Diane wondered if the word "frizzies" had any meaning for her. Probably not.

"But you can't quit, now that you're just beginning to be useful." Philip bit his tongue, and wished he could recall the phrase. Diane was looking coldly at him. After all, it probably wasn't the best way of persuading her to stay on. But, goddammit, didn't she know she was indispensable? Did he have to flatter her, spell it out? Surely she knew he couldn't manage without her.

That evening he calculated what that ill-timed phrase had cost him. In the end Diane had agreed to stay on two days a week for him and he was committed to paying her half her original weekly salary.

Diane, too, was aware what a difference the mean-spirited words had made. Without them, despite Claire, she might have changed her mind about Mitch. But not now.

Diane had gone to Mitch's office, heavy with misgivings and with no greater protection than putting her hair in a bun and wearing really sensible shoes. This nearly did the trick; Mitch took one look at her and knew she wasn't his type. Being a kindly man, he decided on a short interview and a polite dismissal. But after a few minutes he realized Diane had what he thought of as "class" and that she'd be useful for impressing his better type of client. He considered offering her a job as a receptionist, but since he basically associated that position with brassy blond hair and prominent tits, he came up with a better idea. Having once been, for a dramatically short time, a vice president of a studio, he knew the grander the title the less necessity to pay. An "assistant to the producer" did as much shorthand as a secretary and got thirty dollars a week less.

So Diane came home with a bundle of scripts and a job as a story editor to an independent producer. For this she earned a hundred and twenty-five dollars a week cash and could work at home. The girl she'd replaced had been called a reader and got two hundred. One hundred and twenty-five is hardly a living wage, but since office hours did not have to be observed, Diane was free to moonlight. In theory, she had to be available to meet and work with writers as soon as an actual project was set up, but having glanced through the scripts he'd given her she realized this was a distant eventuality. In practice, she spent most of her office time with Mitch rewriting his letters and correcting his grammar.

By making some discreet inquiries among her out-of-work actor friends she soon discovered Mitch could, despite his apparent lack of any kind of talent, afford her salary, such as it was, and pay his rent. He was a classic Indi. Prod. A not too expensive mistake made by the previous management at Mammoth Studios. The mistake in question having been appointing Mitch Vice President in Charge of Production. And he might conceivably still have been there, or at least lasted until the next coup d'etat if somebody hadn't noticed he was operating an inept, though good-natured line of complicated kickbacks from hack writers, in addition to the time-honored system of contributions from producers. Scandal and stockholders suits were to be avoided at all costs, so Mitch negotiated to work out his contract as an independent producer. He would have been unrealistic to imagine his projects would get preferential treatment at the studio, and insane to think his contract would be renewed at the end of his three years.

"Did you get Philip's medicine?"

"Yes. How's he feeling?"

"Awful. Poor sweet."

For a hypochondriac, Philip was lucky with his women. Both Sandy and Diane were adoring and sympathetic. Neither suggested that more Dristan and less whining would make him a more amusing companion.

Diane took the medicine and a glass of water through to the living room where Philip was sprawled out on a sofa, prostrated by what he called a chronic allergy and which Diane had always thought of as hay fever.

"What's Alexandra doing?" he asked.

Diane had last seen Alexandra—or Sandy as she used to be called before the last change of image—about twenty seconds ago, pouring herself a glass of dry white wine, and writing "ninety-six calories" in a little black book she kept for that purpose.

"She's in the kitchen, putting the finishing touches to some canapés."

"Good."

Philip set off toward the kitchen. Something about the tone of his voice, the set of his mouth and a certain purposefulness in his stride made Diane uneasy. In pursuit of Sandy alias Alexandra.

Diane, too, without going so far as to change her name, had had a small change in image. It had begun when she started working for Mitch. Now she could plead lack of time when Sandy asked her to nip down to the market. Philip, who didn't intend to employ anyone to take Diane's place on the days she no longer worked for him, supported her. She learned to say: "Why don't you call Gristedes, they deliver," instead of "Sure, give me the list." As her function changed, so did their attitude. She might still be called upon to pull together the loose ends of some dinner party arrangements, but if they wanted her to make the béarnaise, they damned well had to invite her to dinner. And if there was no one to wash the dishes, that was Sandy's (Diane just couldn't bring herself to call her Alexandra) problem. Diane would say, "Why don't you call the Swedish-American Agency, I always found them very helpful," and go back to her typewriter. Often Sandy ended up doing them herself. Washing dishes might have fitted her gingham and pigtail image, but now she was into black cocktail dresses, called herself Alexandra, affected a cigarette holder, and it was a different story. She longed for a butler, a lady's maid. Diane knew it, and despite herself, could not help taking a small spiteful pleasure in Sandy's discontent. Being in love with Philip herself, she would happily have kept house for

him, and cooked and cleaned and done the whole thing magnifi-
cently on a shoestring. So serve Sandy right if she was foolish
enough to be discontented.

Philip didn't return from the kitchen during the next few minutes, and since it was getting late, Diane went upstairs to the
bedroom where she was going to change her dress and do her
face, "borrowing" Sandy's cosmetics once again in the way she'd
used to, though in more modest surroundings.

The bedroom was now quite different, Sandy's main changes
having been made there: new curtains, a dressing table covered
with pots and lotions and bottles of perfume. It seemed to make
promises, like the advertisements for expensive sheets in the glos-
sy magazines. Buy me, they say, and you will never sleep alone
again. You will wake up to breakfast trays complete with fresh
orange juice and one perfect rose. To exciting telephone calls on
your color coordinated telephone. To the newspaper delivered to
your bedside. Your men will never awake unshaven or in need of
mouthwash. Your women will get up with their hair already
brushed and their skin lightly moisturized. In this bed there is no
risk of hard-to-explain infections, impotency or unwanted preg-
nancies.

In this particular bed, though with different sheets and covers,
of course, Diane had made love with Philip. Just once. Not perhaps up to the standards promised by the advertisements, but
enough to leave her painfully in love.

They didn't have bedrooms like this in Diane's past. The bedroom where her parents had slept had been huge. The furniture
in it seemed small and the distances from the massive Victorian
wardrobe to her mother's dressing table, to the bed, immense.
The bareness of the room emphasized by the carpet stopping for
the final four feet at one end. In winter, and the colder parts of
spring and autumn, Diane's mother went to bed with a woolen
vest under her nightdress. Perhaps that was why Diane was an

only child. By the time she used to creep into their bed in the mornings or after a bad dream, it was warm and comforting. But their sheets, like hers, must have been icy on their cold skins when they slid into bed.

The size, not the temperature, was the difference between her parents' Protestant, Anglo-Irish bedroom and those of Diane's Catholic friends' parents. There, a bed so narrow it seemed not much wider than a single, with a crucifix over it. There would be barely room to squeeze between the bed and the chest of drawers, with its piece of lace, one cheap ornament and a half-used bottle of scent.

And Diane's first room at Oxford. In a boarding house. She used to wake up in her dreary little room, and lie warm in bed, seeing her breath make dragonlike little clouds, and force herself to leap out of bed, cross the linoleum, put a shilling in the meter, light the gas and leap back into bed until the room had warmed a little. When she dressed she would, as she had done as a child, warm each article of clothing before she put it on.

No wonder she loved America, with its promise and opportunities, its "infinite possibilities," its potential for the maximum possible change in the least possible time. Look at Sandy. Six months ago a penniless illegal immigrant, living, however graciously, hand-to-mouth. Now married to an attractive and successful writer, mistress of her own house, safe, happy and in love. It could be Diane, and next time it might be.

Sandy, not looking as though she'd recently counted her blessings, came into the room sniffing, saw Diane and burst into tears.

"Sandy, what's wrong?"

But Sandy, childlike, was unable to make herself understood through her sobs. Diane took her in her arms and patted her back until the large hiccupping motions had subsided.

"What is it? Tell me."

"Philip . . ." and she started again.

"Philip? Has something happened to Philip?"

Sandy shook her head violently.

"Philip did something? Said something?"

Nodding and nose blowing.

"You had a fight?"

"Yes."

"But everything was fine a moment ago. What happened?"

"I was in the kitchen and he just came in and started this stupid fight and we've got guests coming in thirty minutes and look at my face . . ." Sandy crumpled into tears again at the sight of her ruined face and then tried to compose herself so she could repair the damage. She went to the bathroom, followed by Diane, and turned on the cold faucet.

"He just started a fight? Out of nowhere?"

"Oh, about money, as usual. It's so boring, sometimes I think it's all he thinks about. I hate people who spend all their time thinking about money."

Diane said nothing. She spent a lot of her time thinking about money because she didn't have much and it was a day-to-day problem, involving a surprising amount of choices, decisions and end-of-month juggling. Philip thought about it because he was, in fact, not very generous and was now bearing the brunt of Sandy's extravagance. As a past fellow sufferer, Diane felt a certain sympathy toward him. Sandy never thought about it.

"But what an odd moment to pick, just before a party. Surely something must have happened to start it off?"

"Well, yes, but it's such a stupid thing. It's about twenty dollars. How petty can you be?"

"Twenty dollars?"

Considering the sums of money involved in the previous row, twenty dollars was a drop in the ocean. Last time Philip had gone over his accounts and found that Sandy had spent three thousand

84

dollars on clothes and knickknacks during the previous six weeks. There had been shouting, tears, threats to discontinue credit cards, a reconciliation and, eventually, an arrangement, negotiated with Kissinger-like skill by Diane, whereby Sandy would have a hundred and fifty dollars a week to spend on whatever she liked. Anything charged had to be requested and approved by Philip. Both sides emerged outwardly content, but inwardly resentful. Philip congratulated himself on his generosity, his indulgence toward his child bride. His child bride, conditioned by Mom, considered herself the most frugal, the most undemanding of wives.

"Yes. He found a bill . . . I mean, that's really snooping— looking in my private papers—it was for that antique nightdress I bought, you know the one . . ."

"Yes, yes," Diane said, cutting Sandy off before she could embark on a *Vogue* oriented tangent.

"Well, there was the most beautiful shawl, really old and embroidered and the sort of thing you don't often see. I knew if I didn't get it then it would be gone by next week so I put a deposit on it. That's all. And Philip was an absolute beast about it. And started going on about electricity and stuff like that."

"Electricity?" Something had been left out, censored, whatever.

"Do you think you could be an angel and talk to Philip while I try and do something with my face? And deal with any guest who's fool enough to turn up on time. Some of Philip's friends can be a tiny bit literal about invitations."

Sandy pressed a cold washcloth to her face, firmly ending the conversation and dismissing Diane before being questioned any further.

Diane went downstairs, faintly aware that she was only halfway through her own makeup and hadn't really had a chance to do all she wanted to her hair. She didn't look forward to seeing

85

Philip, who presumably wasn't in the happiest of moods, and she disliked getting involved in his and Sandy's private affairs. Nothing changes, she thought, it's like me sitting with Richard while Sandy gets ready, only she married this one.

"How's my rival, your other employer?"

"Oh, fine. He's all excited about some new script he's just found, something about lethal guinea pigs escaping from a lab, and breeding in the way only guinea pigs do."

Philip laughed.

"I don't know. If Alexandra doesn't cut down on her clothes-buying, I'll have to try my hand at something like that myself."

"That's one of the disadvantages of elopements. You don't have time to pack carefully."

In fact, Sandy hadn't taken much with her in the way of loot. She might be extravagant, but she was in no way acquisitive. She had, regretfully, left behind the few pieces of good jewelry given to her by Mom and Dennis, and since she had left in a hurry she had taken only as many of her favorite clothes as she could fit into one large suitcase. At the back of her mind she'd thought she could have them sent on afterward. What good would they be to anyone else? But she'd never quite plucked up the courage to call Mom and ask for them, and now the moment seemed to have passed. Anyway, she was into a new look now.

An uneasy silence descended upon them. Philip picked up *The New York Review of Books* but didn't read it, just held it, a combination security blanket and reminder that he was an intellectual.

"How is she?"

"She seemed very upset, but she's all right now."

"Did she tell you what it was about?"

"Sort of. I got the gist of it, but there was something I didn't understand about electricity."

"It probably wasn't the ideal moment to bring it up, but since I was on the subject, I asked if there was any reason for the light over the washing machine in the basement to burn day and night like some kind of fucking fluorescent eternal flame."

Diane laughed and Philip felt reassured. Up to then he'd been thinking perhaps he'd been a little rough on Alexandra. He began to smile, then she came into the room, beautiful and calm and they both, almost guiltily, stopped laughing.

"Isn't she the sweetest thing you ever saw?"

Diane stroked the kitten in Sandy's hands with the tip of one finger.

"She's very pretty. Where did she come from?"

"She's an Abyssinian. Look at the exotic shape of her ears."

"I meant . . ."

"I saw her in a pet shop and fell in love with her. She's got a pedigree as long as your arm, and . . ." Sandy tailed off and Diane mentally completed the sentence for her. And cost a fortune, and how were they going to break it to Philip.

Philip. He was waiting for her. She'd just come to the kitchen for a fresh pot of coffee and to empty the ashtrays. A five-minute break in the middle of the backbreaking, eye-straining, grueling task of correcting galleys. A tedious job even if done a piece at a time, and exhausting if done virtually all at once. Philip had wanted to add an extra scene, and now if he wanted to make his publication date he would have to return the corrected galleys in two days, which made it a marathon task for him and Diane.

"Where's Philip?"

"In the study. I'd better get back. Why don't you give her some milk? Did you get her a tray?"

"A tray?"

"You know. And some sand or cat litter?"

"Oh, I forgot."

Naturally. And hoped someone else would do it.

"You'd better get something. Philip won't be thrilled if there's an accident."

"Oh, all right, and maybe you'd just mention to him . . . ?"

"I will."

Diane went back to work, bearing coffee and the not very welcome news. Anticipating his reaction. Irritation at the extravagance. Fear of allergy. Her response that it would be something for Sandy to do. His, that there was plenty to do around the house just that second. Galleys to be checked for one. And neither of them saying that letting Sandy check a proof would be an invitation to every writer's nightmare. A bloomer immortalized by one of the little joke pieces at the bottom of a column in the *New Yorker*.

"Come shopping with me."

"What?"

"I'm going shopping. Want to come with me? I need lots of new things."

The girl was mad, self-destructive. But brave, no doubt about it. After the two monumental rows about extravagance, and a smaller one about the kitten, Sandy, with a lot more time on her hands now that shopping was out, had moped around the house, bored. And bored. she had felt less and less like doing domestic chores. There was no fun in devoting the morning to the perfect salad Nîçoise with the perfect flower arrangement in the middle of the table if Philip grunted he wasn't hungry, just leave his in the fridge. And suddenly there was no one to dress up for. She lay around listlessly, slept more than usual, took to eating candies. Diane noticed she seemed to have put on weight. Usually when Sandy detected signs of an extra pound or two it was news, and the pros and cons of various diets were weighed up. But now she didn't seem to care. An expensively bound complete edition of

The Remembrance of Things Past had been bought during her more extravagant days (it was one of the things Philip had screamed about), and she could be seen lying on the sofa, complaining of not feeling well, with Volume One on her lap, as she stared into space. Diane was still jealous of her, thought her silly, but felt sorry for her. She meant no harm, she was just a spoiled child. Gradually Diane started to do small things to amuse her, left her copy of *Vogue*, repeated minor pieces of movie gossip heard at Mitch's office, tried to interest her in the garden, suggested recipes. And also to protect her, checking the contents of the fridge so that Philip didn't have to exist entirely on Sandy's frequently indigestible cooking. Indigestion made him short-tempered and Diane realized her uneventful evenings in front of the television set were often cheerier than Sandy's.

And now Sandy wanted to go shopping.

"But what will Philip . . . ?"

"It's all right." From the tone of satisfaction in her voice, not unlike the tone in which she'd announced her marriage, Diane deduced she had a card up her sleeve. But hard to imagine what. Maybe she'd come into money, but she wouldn't have been able to keep that to herself. Maybe Philip had, but Diane had access to his accounts, and knew he was feeling less flush than usual. Whatever it was, she'd know soon enough. Sandy was obviously bursting to tell her something. An hour and a half later it all became clear. Sandy had bought two or three light, loose, floral dresses. At first Diane thought this was just part of a new look, a new image. Misty-eyed, Laura Ashley innocence. But then they visited the maternity department. Since Sandy was still slimmer than she was, Diane expected some surprised reaction from the saleswoman. None was forthcoming, and Diane realized this was a large part of their sales, to first-time young mothers. When the woman was out of earshot, Diane kissed Sandy and congratulated her, though with a feeling of dismay. A baby would make

89

the marriage real. In the back of her mind she had always, almost subconsciously, hoped the marriage would fade away, turn out to have been only a game. Already, after a few months, Sandy was bored and Philip irritated. Diane, while acting as a buffer and go-between, reproved herself for taking pleasure in the unromantic atmosphere of the house. But a baby was more real than a registry office marriage. A divorce took only a few days in Mexico, but a child could reasonably be expected to stick around for sixteen or seventeen years.

"How long have you known?"

"Since yesterday."

"Is Philip excited?"

"Oh, I haven't told him yet."

"When's it due?"

"As far as I can make out, December."

So Sandy was three weeks pregnant, more or less. And this pregnancy had already cost Philip something in the region of six hundred dollars. More, if Sandy decided to take both the maternity bathing suits. Diane had never seen her swim. It would also, of course, cost him a great deal more if he ever tried to cut his losses and get a divorce.

"How could you be so totally irresponsible?"

Not Philip attacking Sandy, but Claire giving Diane hell.

"What do you mean? You can't imagine I put her up to it."

"You should have known better. Put saltpeter in their gin. You should have stopped it somehow. This kind of thing's bad for the breed."

"Saltpeter?"

"Or whatever it is they're supposed to put in soldiers' coffee. You know. Can you imagine what the child will be like? Probably a combination of the worst qualities of both of them. Though damned if I know what the best qualities might be."

"I suppose it could be pretty and clever."

"Fat chance. Do you suppose they did it on purpose?"

"As far as I could make out Philip was astonished. I mean, I think he assumed she was taking care of all that. And she'd assumed after you were married you started having a series of dear little babies. I opened some champagne, not entirely for selfish reasons. I could see he needed a drink. We drank to the baby's health. She blushed quite prettily. I think when he gets used to the idea he'll be pleased. She's having the time of her life. Lots of sleeping in, little nourishing snacks on trays. Not carrying anything heavier than a handkerchief. Having the spare room done over as a nursery."

"Just remember, diaper changing is not part of your job."

Sandy screamed. Not only because of the pain, which was extreme, but in anticipation of greater pain with the next contraction. And to get some sympathy or attention, at least.

She had never felt more helpless. It was the first time in her life that she did not have some advantage. She was anonymous, just another body on a production line. Up to now she'd always had an edge. Even in situations designed to eliminate privilege. Like at school. But the ugly convent uniform had only emphasized Sandy's natural beauty, and the nuns, while trying to be impartial, couldn't help doting on the sweetest, most charming little girl they'd had. And so good at embroidery, and playing the piano, and sewing, and singing. Not a child who scored the highest grades, but better to be good, sweet child, and let she who can be clever. Even other women who might have been jealous of her beauty were immediately captivated by her charm. Claire was the only one who had been able to resist her.

And now she was just another piece of meat. Competent nurses attended her, but this special and terrifying moment in her life was just part of their everyday routine. And to make it more impersonally nightmarish, none of them spoke English as a first language. So far she had appealed to one Oriental and two girls that she imagined must come from the Philippines. Their faces were impassive, and she wasn't sure whether it was inscrutability, or whether they had a different attitude toward childbirth. After all, they'd thought nothing of their mothers giving birth, at home, in no way disturbing the routine of the household.

She screamed again, for good measure. Her nurse came back into the room. Undernourished, in a thin white nylon uniform, tired.

"I called again. The doctor's on his way. When he arrives he'll give you a shot. I'm sorry, I'm not allowed to."

She handed Sandy some kind of inhaling device. It didn't stop the pain, but it stopped her minding it. Moved her above it in some odd way. Disassociated her from her body. Which was fine for now, but it wasn't going to work when the baby started to come. What if the doctor didn't arrive in time? She was trapped. No, much worse than trapped. Trapped meant she was enclosed in something. But what was happening now was there was something enclosed in her. Something huge, and struggling to get out. She was about to be torn apart. The pain was almost unbearable, and wouldn't, couldn't, stop until it had gotten much, much worse. At least she had no fear that they were Catholics, and would sacrifice her to save the baby. Although now she would gladly make a deal to die, if only the pain would stop. Someone had to help her. A new wave of pain caught her by surprise.

"Diane," she screamed. "Diane, help me. Please."

Diane looked in her purse for change. Seventy cents.

"D'you have a quarter?"

Philip looked at her as though she'd taken leave of her senses.

"A quarter?" he repeated. It seemed a unit of currency he'd

never heard of. As though she'd casually asked him to advance her six yen against her salary next Friday.

"Yes."

He looked at her vaguely.

"In your pocket? Do you have any change?"

Still he didn't seem to catch her drift.

"Alexandra . . . ?" he said.

"Yes. The nurse said it might be hours. She's only in the early stages of labor. And we're down to our last three cigarettes. I thought I'd go look for a machine."

"In a hospital?"

"Sure. All doctors chain-smoke. Usually nonfilter. Haven't you noticed?"

But Philip wasn't to be diverted. In the end Diane went to the cafeteria and bought a carton.

Chapter Five

"I don't believe it. I really don't. She's out getting laid and you're left holding the baby."

"The baby, or Tania, as I prefer to call her, since she has a name and I'm her godmother, is asleep in my bedroom and no trouble or inconvenience to me. And Sandy isn't getting laid. She's out to lunch."

For once Claire spared Diane her usual obligatory joke about the baby's name—speculations on Sandy's radical political affiliations, possibilities of a brief Patty Hearst period—and continued.

"The guy isn't an idiot. He's not going to spring for a lunch at La Côte Basque if she's not going to put out afterward. He's an international bridge player and she's too dumb to shuffle a pack of cards."

"Come on. She's a pretty girl and he's pleased to be seen with her. She deserves a break, she's going stir crazy. It'll do her good to get out. Anyway, as Dostoyevsky has told us, gamblers don't fuck."

"Oh, yeah. You can tell he never worked the Vegas run. Last

time I did some drunken high roller tried to drag me into the john."

"You may be right. It was only last week Philip explained to me that Anatomy is Fate doesn't just mean pretty girls have a better time."

But now she had lost Claire.

Sandy came back from lunch flushed and happy and an hour and a half late. She found Diane at the typewriter knocking off a quick synopsis of a B picture which depended rather too heavily on plagiarism. Tania was crawling around on the floor following the cat, who was effortlessly but carefully keeping one step ahead of her.

"Hello, tweetums. Hello, Ariadne."

Neither the child nor the cat acknowledged her arrival. Ariadne, now rechristened Dennis by Diane and Claire, had come to live with them soon after Tania was born. Sandy's fear of the cat smothering the baby had been encouraged by Philip, who sneezed every time the cat came into the room.

"Did you miss your Mummy?" Sandy asked, trying again to get the child's attention.

"She was a bit grouchy when she woke up from her nap but Claire read to her and soon she was as happy as a clam."

Claire looked as though she would have preferred to continue her pretense of not being interested in Sandy's daughter, and muttered something about keeping the little bastards happy being a whole course at airline school. Then she disappeared into her bedroom, disregarding Sandy's effusive and completely sincere thanks.

"I don't think Claire likes me."

Now was not the time to congratulate Sandy on a rare moment of perception.

"No, that's just her manner. And she adores Tania."

95

Sandy picked Tania up, hugged her, and settled down with her on the sofa, slipping one finger into the diaper to check it.

"She's dry. Claire changed her five minutes ago. How was lunch? Did he teach you to mark cards or anything?"

"It was lovely. Going out to lunch at La Côte Basque makes me feel so glamorous. All that delicious food and everyone looking so smart."

It didn't take much to make Sandy happy. Diane thought how foolish it was of Philip not to make more of an effort to entertain her. If he let her dress up once a week and took her somewhere that really impressed her, she'd be happy enough playing child bride, or wife of eminent novelist, or sophisticated hostess or whatever this month's role was. Provided, of course, he joined in a little, ate her ambitious dishes with enthusiasm the week she was being a gourmet cook, admired the results the week she was into flower arrangements. But he was preoccupied and she was bored. It wasn't surprising; she was twenty-three years old, and might reasonably expect to have some fun, to spend some time with people her own age. But when they entertained, it was usually Philip's contemporaries, one of whom turned out to be this bridge player.

"I'm glad you had fun."

"Yes. That reminds me. Could I possibly leave Tania with you on Friday, for the afternoon? I've never been to the races in America and Joe says he'll take me to Belmont."

"I'd love to have Tania, but do you think that maybe . . . are you sure it's wise?"

Sandy laughed.

"Don't worry. He's sweet, but he's going back to London on Saturday."

Diane laughed too, affectionately. She had mixed feelings about Sandy's independence. She could not allow herself to be put in the position of making alibis for Sandy while she dated other men. On the other hand, it was good for Sandy to get out of the house and if she was doing something inexpensive and harmless, Diane was more than happy to baby-sit.

The next time Sandy dropped the baby off, it was even more innocent. She was spending time with two attractive and amusing homosexuals. It irritated Philip to have them around the house, under his feet. But nothing like as much as it irritated three or four beautiful and successful women who depended on, and fought for, the same time, who needed them as presentable, but not compromising, escorts. Sandy was having a good time with them, lots of little outings and plenty of gossip. And they were enchanted by her. They were seen everywhere together. Sometimes even, in the evening, with Philip. Sandy gave a series of little dinner parties for them.

"Diane, do you have a moment to spare before you go?"

Diane looked up from her work, smiled at Philip.

"Sure."

She was compiling a list of deductible expenses from his checkbook, bills and the household accounts. She didn't get up although she was seated at Philip's desk. She leaned back in the chair, drew on her cigarette, coolly watching him as he perched on the edge of the desk. She sensed he was uncomfortable. Wanted something of her.

"Do you want a drink?" he asked.

"Thanks. I'd love a glass of sherry."

He hesitated for a moment, then when Diane did not move, he got up and poured them both a drink. She watched him. It was forty-five minutes past the time she usually went home, and whatever little chore he had lined up for her would now be done was a favor, not a duty.

He glanced at her, and she was aware he was thinking back to the now-distant afternoon he'd taken her to bed. Also aware that she was now more attractive than she had been then. She knew he was not about to suggest a repeat. Just that he was puzzled by her new confidence. The way she looked. Her sudden ability to maintain a silence, let it be his problem, instead of rushing in to fill a conversational gap.

Diane knew she looked good. She had lost weight and had had her hair well cut. And now she was fairly well dressed, thanks partly to the modest increase in her income, and partly to Sandy. Diane was too proud to ask advice, but she knew how to watch and learn. The result was spectacular.

Mitch was to thank for a lot of it. Diane could see he thought she was classy and intelligent, and realized she'd hit some kind of rock-bottom with Philip. There she was allowing herself to be a secretary cum parlor maid, underpaid, devoid of respect or thanks, being, without a murmur of apology, asked to witness the honeymoon scenes of the man she was in love with. She became coldly, quietly angry. Partly with herself, but mostly with Philip. She still loved him, but she didn't like him. It was hard to.

"It's about Alexandra and those fags."

"Yes?"

"Can you do something? Speak to her? I can't stand them around the house all the time. Don't they have jobs or homes to go to? Francis was here for dinner three times last week."

Francis did have a job to go to, he was a very successful interior decorator. He'd had one good idea and parlayed a very modest talent into a respectable living. He didn't, in fact, have much of a home to go to, living in a small apartment with plenty of closet space, somewhere to sleep and change clothes. The rest of his life was spent in public places or other people's houses.

"But she's fond of them, they're her friends. It . . . well, it gives her something to do."

"She doesn't need something to do. She's got me and a child and a house to run."

"I know. But she needs some fun. Some friends. She needs to get out."

"If she'd make a little more effort with my friends . . . they're interesting people. Not like those two giggling pansies."

"Sandy's very young, it's good for her to have someone to giggle with."

"Maybe, but I don't want them under my feet, making themselves at home in my house, helping themselves to my cigars."

"I'll talk to her. She's bringing Tania over tomorrow."

"Sandy's bringing Tania over tomorrow morning. For a couple of hours, okay?"

Diane sounded defensive. Claire made her feel guilty for allowing the apartment to be used as a day-care center. Which was silly, because, if unobserved, Claire spent more time playing with Tania than Diane did.

"Just make sure she remembers to pick her up—remember what happened with her cat. Anyway, I'm leaving at eleven."

Terrific. That meant she could have a nice cozy chat with Sandy. Not that she actually meant to lecture her on her new friends, and Philip's disapproval of them. She thought that considering the amount of attention Philip had to spare for Sandy, he was lucky her new men friends were homosexual.

"Have you put your hair in curlers to make me feel at home as we eat, or are you going out later?" Claire asked.

"Sorry, it is a rather revolting sight, but I've got a date later and I reckoned you'd sooner I cooked than beautified."

"Who with?"

"Oh, just Dan. I'm having a drink with him later."

"Who?"

"You know, Dan."

"Oh, Dan. Mr. Goodbar."

"As opposed to your own casual dates, every one of them a prince."

"At least I make the turkeys buy me a hot meal once in a while."

"Listen, I don't go out with married men. Which leaves fags and that new category—men who drug themselves into impotence. And Dan. I'll settle for him as he is. Flowers would be nice, so would candlelight dinners. But this is New York in the eighties."

"Drink?" Dan's question suggested a negative response would be in order. "Or d'you want to wait till we get to my place?"

"I'd love a brandy."

Dan didn't grudge her the price of a brandy. Not so long as she didn't linger over it. He hadn't, in fact, ever asked her to have dinner with him. He knew their relationship wasn't based on food and conversation. And Diane could imagine the hour and a bit of embarrassment and inhibition that would face them if they were ever to embark on such a socially ambitious evening. Sure they could talk, but in bed, afterward. That was easy. The drink was a matter of principle. Tonight, after lying through shame to Claire, she insisted he go through the formality of buying it for her.

"Okay, if you're finished, let's go."

Well, that was about ten minutes of date before the sex part started. Which made sense. God knows, they had nothing to say to one another. Diane didn't even really like him. They met to fuck, so why was she now resentful that he never made an even faintly romantic gesture. But if she didn't like him, let alone love him, why had she been anxious and occasionally tearful when he once hadn't called for a week. Only because she was lonely, she told herself.

* * *

100

"He's wonderful, Diane. If only you could see him. His big sad eyes.

"But, Sandy . . ."

"Oh, I know, darling. But there's nothing to worry about. It's all completely innocent, and he loves me so."

"But you're married. Doesn't he know?"

"Of course he knows. That's why he's so sad. And he's *so* poor."

Diane breathed a sigh of relief. Sandy was in no way avaricious but, in truth, it wasn't likely that she'd run off with a pauper, no matter how big his sad eyes.

"He sounds Russian. Is he?"

"No, of course not, don't be silly. He's Scottish and his mother's a direct descendant of Bonnie Prince Charlie. He drinks too much, and, for your information, he's never tried to lay a hand on me."

"All right, Thursday night would be fine."

"Do you want to bring anybody?"

"Mitch's my only contact in the industry, and I don't suppose you'd want him."

Sandy shuddered.

"No, I was only joking. But let's see who we can round up who could help."

"We'll make Philip invite someone from a magazine who could buy an article or two. And someone from a studio. Wouldn't it be wonderful if I could get him a script to write?"

Diane sighed. Poor Philip. Still, the two pet fags were out. Now the question was whether Philip would welcome a series of lame ducks as an alternative. Probably not.

"She's gone."

"What do you mean?"

"Alexandra has left me."

Diane looked around her. The room was like a parody of one occupied by a deserted man. The ashtrays were full, the bottle on the table empty. Dirty glasses and a couple of plates on the floor, Philip gray, tired and unshaven.

"Where's Helga?" Not that it mattered, but this mess should be cleaned up.

"Oh, she's with Tania."

"Tania?"

"Yes, they're watching *Sesame Street*."

"Tania's here?"

"Of course."

"You mean Sandy didn't take her with her?"

Philip just looked at her uncomprehendingly. Diane decided to let it go. In fact, it was hard to decide whether she would have been more shocked by Sandy eloping with Tania in tow, or leaving the child, behind, abandoned.

"Where did they go?"

"Paris."

"But I thought Godfrey was broke. I mean, I know you helped him get work, but it can't have paid very much. And Alexandra . . ."

"What has Godfrey got to do with this? If he's had any part . . ."

He tailed off; Diane was silent. She'd assumed Godfrey was the man Sandy had run off with. So who could it be? Paris. Made an impulsive dash to see the collections with her designer friends? No, obviously not. Philip would be angry and outraged, not broken. It had to be a romantic running off. He'd been replaced by another man. But who?

"Philip, I'm having trouble getting this straight. Sandy has . . . er . . . left you. Right?"

"Right."

"She's gone to Paris?"

"Yes."

"Who with?"

"John Taylor."

"John Taylor?"

"Yes."

"Who's he?"

"I don't know. Don't you?"

"No."

"Nobody seems to. Or if they do, they're not admitting it."

"Do you know anything about him?"

"Not much. Nothing good. Someone said he was an entrepreneur. Christ knows what shady dealings that term covers. He seems to have money, I don't know how much. His name has been 'linked' with those of a couple of minor actresses. His reputation isn't good."

"Oh, dear."

"I don't know what to do."

Of course he didn't, and as usual he assumed she should. Help him get Sandy back? That seemed, at the moment, impossible. And the thought was, she couldn't help being aware, pleasing. Not an emotion she was proud of. But no woman, not even those later canonized, could resist a moment of joy, seeing a man who had tortured her, suffer himself. If only he hadn't been such a clichéd fool in the first place. All right, she would gloat in private later. And it would be a meaningless triumph. Instead of Sandy's presence in the house and her knowledge that he was less than happy, she would now have to put up with the new stream of ideal cover girls, of imagining their halcyon days, or nights.

"Well, first of all, we've got to do something about Tania. I'd better go and see if Helga wants to be promoted to nanny, at least on a temporary basis. Whatever happens, you'll need live-in help for a while."

"Will I?"

"Don't worry about it. You've got enough on your mind at present. Let me see what I can do."

And Diane set about putting the household back on its feet. Lying to the appalling Helga. Cleaning up Sandy's mess.

Chapter Six

"What's all this I hear about your little friend Sandy?"

"I don't know. What is it?" Diane saw no reason to tell Mitch anything he didn't already know about one of her friends. Also, she was discouraged by the prurient interest which she felt was all around her, the disapproving joy with which the news of Sandy's elopement, or Philip's humiliation, was greeted.

"I hear she's left her husband."

"Yes."

"How come?"

"I don't know. I was as surprised as you are. They seemed happy enough. I suppose it was too dull for her. She's young, probably she was bored. She had nothing real to do." Diane groped for an American phrase which she could use to communicate Sandy's tentative groping for some kind of meaning or activity in her life. "I think she wanted to be a person in her own right."

Mitch snorted, that was the only word for it. "Well, it's too late for that now. There's a child to be considered."

Diane was silent.

"Isn't there?"

"Well, yes."

"So what're you going to do?"

"It's not really up to me." Diane said, her voice trying to suggest that if it wasn't entirely her business, it was absolutely none of his.

"Well, someone has to do something. It'll probably be you. Besides, you have eyes for him. Now's your chance."

Diane's expression should have been enough to freeze Mitch solid, but he continued undeterred.

"Look, here's a guy. His wife has left him. He's got a small kid. He's not going to look after it himself. He's got to be looking for someone. And soon. And those chicks he used to go around with aren't going to be any help."

To Diane's certain knowledge Mitch had never met Philip, let alone been introduced to any of his former girl friends. But Mitch was saying out loud what she tried not to think about, even alone in the small dark hours of a sleepless night.

"You're impossible. Sandy has only been gone a week. It's more than likely she'll come back . . ."

"You've heard from her?"

"No, but she may well patch things up with Philip. *And* she's a good friend. *And* they're still married."

Diane had first embarked on *Remembrance of Things Past* when she'd been up at Oxford but, between studying and a social life, she hadn't got very far. Now she lay on Sandy's sofa, engrossed in Sandy's beautiful leather-bound set. Swann and Odette, Saint-Loup and Rachel. For an hour or two every afternoon they became more real than the hot, noisy New York street outside.

Tania, a chubby, contented little girl, slept for two hours after lunch each day. The nap time could have been used by Diane to

106

read any of a number of appalling scripts submitted to Mitch. But she had decided these were her two hours of peace and comfort. Her time out. Philip didn't complain. She often slept at the house now, in the nursery. Helga wasn't much of a stopgap, and Philip wasn't the man you'd choose to put the final polish on Tania's toilet training. From time to time she took the child back to the apartment for the night. Her social life, or to be more specific, her sex life, was now planned some time in advance. Some time when Helga was committed to sleeping over. She kept it simple, spent very little time on it. Dan, once or twice a week. Sometimes a substitute for Dan. She wasn't going to let sexual frustration do anything destructive to the new balance of power in Philip's household. Now she ran the household, efficiently and firmly. Helga knew she was onto a good thing, and when Diane gave her instructions, they were carried out. Most of Diane's reading for Mitch took place at Philip's house, usually late at night. She would sit on the end of Tania's bed, skimming through a script, until the child's eyes closed and her thumb fell out of her tiny mouth.

Diane slept a good deal less and lost weight. She was pale and there was no time to go to the hairdresser's, so her hair was tied back in a sort of bun. Her time was rationed, and her expression became alert, severe, suspicious of anything that would waste an hour. The result was surprising. Without being beautiful, she gained a kind of elegance along with her look of authority. Now she was never tentative, and she noticed that people listened when she spoke.

"This is it. This is the one. We're rich."

"We?" Diane knew of no percentage coming to her of this, she imagined, illusionary windfall.

"I've done it. You'll see."

107

Diane had heard this kind of optimistic exuberance from Mitch in the past. It had led to nothing and, while she wished him well, she now retained her calm.

Usually the script or property ceased to be mentioned after a day or two, and to bring the subject up was tactless. This time, however, the mood and the elation continued. Twice when she came in to collect or return scripts she found him in the middle of negotiation. The second time she realized the terms being discussed were quite different and definitely more favorable than the first.

"What's happened, Mitch? New studio interested?"

"Yes, I've got the two of them at each other's throats."

"You're conducting some kind of auction?"

"No, I've told them what I want. No negotiating. The first unconditional yes gets the movie."

"But there seemed to be some difference between the figures you were discussing today and what I heard you talking about on Tuesday."

"Yes, well, I'm not asking exactly the same deal from both the interested parties. It'll cost Mammoth two hundred thousand more up front than MGM." He smiled in a self-congratulatory way.

"How come? And do they know about the difference? And anyway, doesn't Mammoth have first call on anything you come up with?"

"I told them it would cost them more. Teach them to respect their betters. I took a lot of shit from that studio in my time."

As Diane understood it, he'd taken a good deal more than shit. Petty cash and bribes, for instance. But she held her peace.

"You're due for a promotion. I can use you full time on the movie. Pay you well too, at least let *them* pay you well. Write you into my deal, give you a credit. Teach the bastards a lesson."

* * *

Sandy lay on the sofa, a glass of champagne in one hand, the other stretched delicately out to the manicurist. On her lap was the latest British copy of *Vogue*. Lovely to think she could just skim through and decide what she wanted to buy. And Claridges. The name summed it all up. She'd only been in the hotel once before, when a rich cousin had had a coming-out party, and Sandy had had a brief taste of what being a debutante was like. A strong enough taste for her to have referred to the party as one of a series, to have given John the impression that she had, in fact, been a debutante. Well, she hadn't actually lied, and it wasn't as though lots of debs didn't come from less good families than she did. Richer, that was all.

She wished John would wake up. She'd had her hair done downstairs, and when she'd come up again she'd rustled about, trying to wake him accidently-on-purpose. But he'd just grunted and turned over. So she'd sent for the manicurist. Save her time later on, and no point in him seeing her doing all the stuff necessary to stay beautiful. Then when he woke up she'd be ready to go out to lunch, maybe go shopping afterward. Buy something beautiful for this evening. She needed some new stuff. Had to keep up with John's friends. They didn't see any of hers, and he hadn't shown any curiosity to meet them. Just as well. She'd changed a lot since she'd lived in London. They'd all seem very young to her now. And John's crowd was very sophisticated. It would be hard to imagine introducing him to her family. Even if her family didn't think she was happily married in New York. In time she would have to introduce them, of course. But better get the divorce settled first. She wondered what Philip was doing now.

She signed the manicurist's bill, added the tip to it. She hadn't changed her francs into pounds. Didn't seem worth it. Easier to sign.

* * *

109

Philip came into the kitchen, took another beer from the refrigerator. Diane was standing by the stove, watching something boil.

"Quenelles? Coq au vin?"

"No, just boiling Tania's bottle. Hygiene isn't Helga's strongest point. Are you hungry?"

"Not really." But now that she mentioned it, suddenly he was. He hadn't eaten a real meal in some time. Either he had made himself sandwiches, or had eaten rich restaurant meals in the line of duty. Now he craved something simple, but hot, on the kitchen table.

"I was going to scramble some eggs. Would you like some? Or an omelette?"

"That sounds good. What kind?"

"My special. A Diane omelette. Trust me."

She opened the refrigerator, started to root around. Philip immediately felt better. There was something very comforting about watching a woman cook, especially when she did it effortlessly, not making a huge production of it like Alexandra. Alexandra always took two or three hours to prepare the simplest meal. It had always been delicious, but ornate, an occasion requiring congratulations and effusive compliments. He watched Diane put the bread in the oven to warm, then chop up the bacon, put it in the pan, keeping an eye on it as she chopped up the green onions and added them. Then she sliced tomatoes and mushrooms, left them on one side as she set the table, simply but neatly. Not a trace of Alexandra's cunningly folded napkins here. Thank God, because now he was really hungry. Diane added the stuff on the table to the pan, seasoned it, then beat up the eggs in a bowl.

"Open the wine, would you? It's almost ready."

The eggs sizzled in the hot butter, the edges curling up, slightly brown. It smelled delicious. Diane tipped in the filling, neatly flipped over the omelette, cut it in two, put each piece on a warm plate and carried the food over to the table. Philip poured the wine as she put the hot bread down.

"God, that tastes good. I was starving, I didn't know you could cook."

"I can't, really. At least nothing complicated. But I can manage with most of the stuff I like. Spaghetti mainly."

"You'll make someone a good wife someday."

A commercial came on and Claire got up and went into the kitchen to refill her glass.

"Do you think in ten years' time we'll be sitting here, just like this? Drinking beer and polishing our nails?" she asked on her return.

"Probably. If you mean you and me sharing this slum and waiting for the telephone to ring. I'm not so sure I'm good for another ten years of Johnny Carson, though."

"I remember once when I was eighteen, I said to a girl friend that if I wasn't married by the time I was twenty-one, I'd kill myself. Then suddenly twenty-one didn't seem like automatic senility. And each year I say, now I'm in my prime. My luck will change."

"And more and more often I think that what a man wants in a wife isn't virginity and firm thighs. I tell myself it's a sense of humor, or the ability to mix a great martini. What he really wants is a mature woman, and that means bags and lines."

"And our patron saint is Jeanne Moreau."

"And we're already more than halfway through our lives. I mean, no one really expects to find passion and domestic bliss before the age of ten. Nor after the age of fifty."

"Make that sixty, will you?"

"It's a deal."

"But we'll be sitting here, when you're not scrubbing Philip's kitchen floor. At least you've got job security. I'll probably be a waitress in a diner. You'll still be carrying a torch for him and I'll be complaining about being stood up by a trucker."

"The final test is how you die. Living alone, there's always tomorrow. But if you die alone, you know you've fucked up somewhere along the line."

"I'll die in a retirement home for airline employees. Hundreds of old crones with fallen arches, immaculate hairdos and frozen smiles. 'There you go,' they'll say, as I go for good."

Fortunately the telephone rang. Diane was relieved. If there was one thing that irritated Claire, it was morbid conversations. On the other hand, if there was one thing that distracted her it was the telephone ringing. In a moment or two Claire would have accused her of being drunk. Something she only complained about when an element of self-pity crept in, not if her companion was merely vomiting or dancing on the table. To these minor lapses she was impervious.

Diane listened to the conversation for long enough to make sure it wasn't for her. It rarely was, but it might have been Dan, drunk and suddenly horny. Anyway, it wasn't.

"It was Bill. He's in town. I'm going over to his hotel. See you tomorrow. Okay if I borrow your green purse?"

"Diane, it's me."

"Sandy. Where are you?"

"Beverly Hills. At the hotel. Are you talking to me?"

"Evidently."

"No, you know what I mean. I was scared to call."

"You don't have to be. I didn't know where you were, otherwise I'd have called or written. Tania's fine. She can count up to four."

"The angel. I miss her so. I can't wait to see her."

"Helga's managing quite well. And I sort of keep an eye on things."

"And Philip?"

"He's okay."

"Very cross?"

"Fairly."

"Oh, well. That was to be expected, but he'll get over it. It wouldn't ever have worked out."

"Well . . ."

"Does Tania miss me?"

"I suppose so. She must."

"I'll be back in a week or so. John has some business in New York."

Just as things were starting to calm down.

It was idiotic to feel guilty. She owed no explanation to Philip, and Sandy was almost her best friend. A depressing thought, and a reflection on her social graces. But it felt odd to be going out to dinner with Sandy and John.

She wasn't the only one who thought it strange. Claire had contented herself with observing that Diane must be out of her fucking mind, but her reticence might have been based on her recurring need for Diane's green purse: "I don't know why I can't find something else to go with my sexy new shoes and if you're going out with *them*, you'll be using your black evening bag."

Mitch, however, had been more disapproving and more specific.

"He's going to fall on his ass. Just make sure you're not there when it happens. Your little friend's going to wake up one morning and find herself in real trouble."

"What kind of trouble?"

"If he's lucky he'll go bankrupt, but I'd say it's more likely he'll face charges of fraud, embezzlement—that kind of thing."

"But he seems to be pretty well-heeled."

"You'll see."

And Diane, dressed in her best, but as usual feeling dowdy beside Sandy, was beginning to see. John had greeted her with enthusiasm, but she had the feeling it was a display of his charm, rather than a reaction to hers. Not for the first time she felt the distrust many men show for the girl friends of their wives or mistresses. It was as though he feared Sandy had told her something compromising about him or that Diane knew, from some outside source, something about him which she might tell Sandy.

Sandy was drinking champagne; a half-empty bottle stood on ice. Diane asked for a whiskey, and John ordered it from room service. He didn't drink, but ordered four Cokes and some hors d'oeuvres. When the order arrived he signed the check, adding a large tip. Diane had the feeling the hors d'oeuvres and the extra Cokes had been added to make the order more substantial. No "one soda and two straws" image about John.

Conversation went slowly, Sandy overanxious that John and Diane should like each other. John guarded. Diane checking him and the room out, seeing nothing to confirm Mitch's forecast of impending gloom. Until they were ready to leave for dinner, and John telephoned to reserve a table, when Sandy said:

"Do we have to go there again? We were there for lunch."

"I like to go where I'm known."

Or where he had a charge account, Diane thought.

"Courtesans. That's what the most intelligent and charming women have always been. Courtesans." Rolling the word around on his tongue, savoring it.

Sandy shifted slightly in her seat. She had heard John expound his "philosophy" before and was unmoved by it, but she was uncomfortable to have Diane hear him showing off. For that was all it was, but nevertheless, he should have had more sense. Also, this kind of thing had sounded better in Europe a month or two ago. Before some of the gilt had worn off. When they'd been more in love and, let's face it, richer. Not that John ever showed any anxiety about money, or had noticeably curtailed his spending. But the areas in which money was being spent seemed smaller to her. Now it was the same hotels, the same stores and the same restaurants.

Courtesans, God help us, thought Diane. Poor little Sandy, having to sit still for this garbage. She wouldn't even think about the feminist aspect. The sheer silliness of it all was enough for her. Sandy was sublimely silly herself, of course, but even so. This speech must be making her cringe.

"Of course, it isn't fashionable to say it nowadays, but that's just hypocrisy. Or maybe you don't agree, Diane?"

Diane smiled coldly, said nothing. Well aware that though John was no doubt accurately expressing his idiotic views of what he called courtesans, he was also baiting her. He could hardly expect a less than beautiful girl to agree with him. She looked helplessly from John to Sandy, and started back again toward John, but halfway, a familiar face, out of context, diverted her. The strangeness of seeing David's face after ten years was heightened by his head being, Cheshire-cat–like, the only part of him showing in the expensively unlit gloom. Celtic twilight, Diane's father would have called it.

"Sorry I'm late," David said. But to John.

"No problem. I'm perfectly happy here with two beautiful women, some wine and intelligent conversation."

So far as Diane could remember neither she nor Sandy had managed to get a word in edgewise, but then again they hadn't tried very hard.

"David, I'd like you to meet our good friend, Diane. She and Alexis used to be roommates."

"Hello, Diane." He shook her hand and greeted her as though

this were the first time they'd met. Adding to the confusion already caused by John's reference to Alexis. Alexis? She'd only just got used to hearing her called Alexandra. Now what?

"Hello," she said in the same tone, taking a lead from him. Was this his way of telling her, for some unknown reason, not to say they'd met before? Maybe . . . surely he couldn't not remember her.

"Were you playing?" Sandy asked, perking up with the arrival of a new and attractive male.

"Yes. That's why I was late. I wanted to get away earlier, but I couldn't leave when I was winning. Had to give him a chance to get his money back."

"And did he?" Diane wanted his attention, to will him to acknowledge her. He looked at her and smiled. A warm but somehow dangerous smile. At that moment she realized he had no memory of having ever seen her before.

"No way," he said.

"Well, now we're all here, let's order. Alexis, what do you feel like?"

Diane picked her menu up gratefully: it gave her a little time to collect herself. She noticed that David left his on the table. Despite herself, she glanced at him. He was giving her the look— the insulting quick-summing-up look of, "I could probably have her if‧ I wanted. Do I? Yes . . . to my surprise I really do . . . so why not?" The quick up-and-down. She pretended not to see, but she was thrilled. After that she never had a chance. She never made a move to save herself. Not even a token gesture of coyness at the end of dinner, when without even a glance of complicity to her, or the hint of it being a question, he said:

"I'll drop Diane home, it's on my way."

Neither Sandy nor John showed any sign of wondering how David knew where Diane lived. Instead, John said:

"Oh, I thought we might have a game or two."

"We're in the company of two beautiful women and you want to play backgammon?"

John looked glum, not able to say his beautiful woman had lost some of her novelty and he didn't consider Diane pretty.

"Why didn't you play him? And don't give me that shit about beautiful women."

"He owes me. There's too much on the tab, if it gets to be any more he'll give up all effort to pay. I can lose, but I can't win. The odds are too long for me."

No reference to the past. Well, she certainly wasn't going to bring it up.

The taxi drew up outside his apartment and Diane got out. He glanced at her as if he expected a "Where are we? Why haven't you taken me home?" standard coy hesitation. But she just waited on the doorstep as he fiddled with his keys.

Upstairs he led her into the living room. She looked around but didn't sit down. He offered her a drink and went into the kitchen to get it. She followed him, looking briefly at a few really bad paintings, and his current reading matter. Two fat dull books, both on the bestseller list. She knew how he would defend having bought them. "A good read, I like something to last me through the summer." Then, defensively: "I read to relax." Unanswerable.

He poured the brandy, waiting for her to protest—"Oh, just a small one for me, that's much too much." She said nothing. He poured them both large drinks. Raised his glass.

"Cheers."

"Cheers," she replied, concealing her dislike of the class-dividing toast.

"Like to see the rest of the apartment?"

She nodded, knowing she was supposed to simulate a keen interest in interior decoration in order to find herself in the bedroom through no fault of her own. She wouldn't play that game with him. She could see he was slightly shaken by her attitude. Somewhere she was beginning to gain his respect. She saw him glance at her again, reevaluating her. Thrown by her outwardly ladylike appearance and her dispensing with the coy niceties of seduction. He mightn't necessarily enjoy them, but they were an expected, accepted part of the game. The few moments in this particular game when the woman had a temporary advantage. And she wasn't going to play.

"The master bedroom," he said.

She looked at it with mild interest, a nondescript room. Dominated by a businesslike, overwide bed and a wall of mirrored closets. Hard to make any comment that didn't include a giggle. Diane moved, unhurriedly, toward the window, which led onto a small terrace. She looked out at a few half-lit office buildings, what passed here for a magnificent view. She decided to skip a comment and by the same token she failed to open the sliding doors and force him to play the seduction scene outside. They both knew it was the normal procedure.

Instead, as he put some poorly chosen pop classic on the record player, she sat straight backed, legs crossed, drink firmly in hand, on the foot of the bed.

He turned from the record player, leaned over and kissed her. Not a passionate kiss, more a kiss which suggested easy intimacy, two grown people who knew the ropes, no big deal.

Diane put her glass on the floor, "body language" for acquiescence. David pushed her back on the bed, so that he ended up lying partly on top, partly to one side of her. Now the kiss was open-mouthed, unabashedly sexual, though more in the nature of the next step on a clearly well-trodden path than a grand overwhelming passion.

One hand slid along her body, not even hesitating on the way, and firmly established itself between her legs

"No."

"You want me to behave myself?" He was more encouraged than not by this semblance of a challenge.

"Of course not. Why else am I here? I just mean don't go so fast. I want it all."

He smiled, and his grip on her relaxed. Diane realized this was going to be far better than she'd expected and infinitely more dangerous.

"All right," he said. "Let's take your dress off."

She stood up, turned her back. He unzipped her slowly. She turned, the black dress hanging from her shoulders, held up by one hand.

"Turn the lights off."

"You're kidding."

"No."

He turned the lights down, quickly got out of his clothes, hanging them casually but carefully over a chair to avoid creases. She undressed, slid into bed with her back to him, so that he never saw her naked. He got into bed with none of her modesty. What were all the jogging, all the morning workouts for, if not to make a good first impression?

"Why so shy?"

"It's been a long time. I looked better, nearly ten years better, the last time we did this."

"Last time . . . ?"

"You really don't remember, do you?"

He said nothing, silencing her with his mouth as he played for time. So he really didn't remember. Not a flattering thought, but she offered no resistance as he folded her into his arms. Instead she sighed and pressed herself against his hard thighs and chest, feeling as she always did, wonder at the difference between the feel of a hairy male body and her own.

"I mean, we've done this before."

119

"I know . . . I just didn't . . ."

"It was a long time ago. A lot of blood's flowed under the bridge since then."

"I'm sorry . . . I . . . give me a clue."

Diane felt an unaccustomed and probably temporary moment of power, but was aware it was a dubious advantage. Apart from a brief moment of embarrassment, presumably the person in the stronger position was the one who forgot, not the one who remembered. But she was excited and part of her was amused by the possibility of teasing him.

"In London. Ten years ago."

The clue didn't seem to help him.

"Sure," he said, but he didn't sound so sure. Instead he seemed thrown, confused. She'd appeared at first to be almost too easy, but at the same time clearly not a tramp. Then she'd become, for a moment, less interesting since it appeared he'd had her before and not found her memorable. Then suddenly very exciting if she only seemed amused and turned on by his having forgotten. And there was also, for a moment, a troubled expression on his face, as though he'd had a premonition of danger. Then it cleared. What harm could one night do?

"Was I a good lover to you?"

"The best."

"Tell me more."

"I don't think I will, maybe it'll come back to you."

"I want to know."

This time it was her arms around his neck, her kiss which halted conversation until their lovemaking moved into a new stage. Now their speech was no longer cool, but urgent and breathless.

"Tell me," he said, sliding down her body until his tongue touched, then licked, then sucked her nipples.

She moaned, but didn't reply.

"Tell me," he insisted.

"Later . . . afterward—"

"No, now."

He was back in control of the situation. Diane's brief moment of advantage had passed with his implied threat that they would go no further until she told him.

"The first time," she said, ". . . the first time, after you picked me up at a party."

Her body moved and pushed and rubbed against him. Her legs parted and she pressed herself, warm and wet and urgent against his belly.

"Yes?" he asked, both teasing and demanding and as full of desire as she was.

"At this party. I was with someone . . ." No need to explain George, nor to think of him, painless though it was, just for once. "You sat down beside me, started to talk. You asked me to dance. I said I didn't know how."

"You couldn't dance?"

"Still can't. You asked me to go away with you for the weekend. To the south of France. I laughed and said of course not, but I knew you meant it. And I was pleased."

An expert, exploring hand was touching her.

"Please, oh please."

"No. First tell me."

"The man I was with, he was a real bastard. I said I was tired, I wanted to go home. He didn't mind, actually he was quite pleased. He was dancing with someone else. You took me back to your hotel and—Please, I want you. I want it."

"And then?"

"There's nothing to tell. We made love—it was wonderful."

"Like this? Like this?"

And at last he was inside her.

"Yes, yes, oh yes."

121

"And like this?"

But it wasn't really the same at all. Last time she'd been nineteen and in love with another man, she'd been lonely and scared but never at loss for a sexual partner. Now she was twenty-nine and—for a moment she'd forgotten Philip. Of course she was in love with another man but she was at a place in her life when the sexual act had some validity, some importance of its own. It didn't depend on being in love, it wasn't a step toward, or away from, getting married. It could be isolated from emotions, from the rest of her life, and it could matter terribly, especially at a time like this, when she hadn't been made love to for some time.

And there was another difference. He was a much better lover now. Perhaps less virile in the six-times-a-night sense, though that remained to be seen. But there was an expertise, a control which left her open and helpless, and at the same time, made her feel expert. Like a highly trained show jumper. She came, which she didn't always do, exactly when he wanted her to, and relaxed, panting, almost sobbing.

That was where the show jumper bit came in. It was like having cleared a high fence, then been reined in, checked, turned and once the stride was right, urged over another fence. Since he never doubted it, never gave her a choice the second—the impossible, second—orgasm was instantly achieved.

She lay with her face against the wet, salty hair on his chest. Listening to his heart.

"I was a little in love with you, you know."

"You were?" Slightly flattered, but his tone said: "That's all in the past, we don't want any sentiment now."

She caught the hint in his voice, and continued in a slightly different direction.

"I still dream about you sometimes."

"Like what?"

"Just your basic erotic dream. Things we did mixed up with fantasies of my own."

"What kind of things?"

But even then she knew she would have to save all that. If she wanted to see him again there would have to be something new each time to keep his attention. She'd have to be a modern-day Scheherazade if she wanted to keep seeing him. And she wanted to keep seeing him.

Chapter Seven

I'm completely happy, Diane thought, staring out the window. A tiny wave of water lapped over the top of her rubber glove, divided and ran down into all the fingers. She took it off, shook it out, wiped her hands on her apron. No dishwashing hands without a wedding ring, is what Claire would have said.

She glanced at Philip, sitting at the breakfast table. He held a book, but wasn't reading it. But neither did he seem to be deep in thought. More pleasantly relaxed. It was probably safe to speak; she was always careful not to interrupt the creative process.

"It's beginning to look as though Mitch's movie's going to go ahead."

"Yes?"

"He's offered me the job of associate producer."

"Really?"

"Just a title, I imagine, but more money. I'll be on their payroll, and he can afford to be generous."

"That's good. How long'll the movie take?"

"Oh, probably six to eight months. That's counting preproduction and there'll still be quite a lot to do during editing. And better still there's talk of a three-picture deal so I may be gainfully employed for a couple of years."

"Hm."

"But I'll still have most weekends free if you need me. For Tania or anything."

Philip looked thoughtful. He opened a magazine, turned a page or two. Diane propped the wet rubber glove up on a tap so that it could dry, took a dishtowel, and started to wipe the silverware in the draining rack.

"Heard from Alexandra lately?"

Diane looked around, but Philip kept his eyes on the magazine.

"Yes, actually, she should be back soon. If it's okay with you I could take Tania to see her. I mean if you don't want her to come up here."

"No. I'd like to see her."

"She's . . . " Oh God, how to say it without hurting him. "John's coming too."

"Good."

"Good?"

"I want to talk to her about a divorce. Makes it easier if there's someone else in the picture."

Food for thought. Diane took a kitchen sponge and began to wipe the sink. There was a short pause and she heard Philip getting up from the table. A moment later she felt his arms around her. She turned her head slightly so that he could see her friendly smile, so that he wouldn't know the feeling he gave her. Every tired, tense muscle in her body relaxed. She forced herself to go on wiping the now clean sink, to pretend to him that she, too, knew this was just a grateful, friendly hug.

"I need to divorce Alexandra, so I can ask you to marry me."

"Oh."

"Will you?"

Diane's first reaction was a small wave of disappointment, almost of resentment. A sense of being shortchanged. Of course, being proposed to by Philip was the culmination of every fantasy, but this wasn't the way it was supposed to happen. She could think of no proposal either in fiction or the movies that had taken place over a kitchen sink. How did real people do it? The only models she could conjure up that moment were Jane Austen characters. Her heroines were always surprised when the moment came, but never disheveled. And a proposal came accompanied by or following a declaration of love. And Philip had made none. She wasn't about to refuse him, but there was no possibility of accepting him without something more.

"Why?" she asked, turning to look him straight in the eye.

He drew in his breath, then said nothing.

"Why don't you sit down?" he asked. He went to the refrigerator and took out a bottle of wine.

She took two glasses from the cupboard and sat at the kitchen table. Philip poured them each a glass. Diane noticed that he'd opened the most expensive, special occasion and celebration wine. And without any apparent hesitation. She gave him full marks for that. Such an extravagant gesture was usually accompanied by some soul-searching and weighing up of the occasion.

"Why do you want to marry me?"

Philip hesitated a second.

"I'm not a romantic, I'm sorry, I've been married twice before. I suppose I should have done this differently—candlelight and flowers and so on. But I'm too old for that. All I can say is I hope you'll marry me. I'll try to be a good husband."

"But . . ."

"You know I care about you and . . ." He tailed off, and when Diane didn't immediately reply, continued: "I need you. I . . . I love you."

Diane's happiness was undiminished even when, after the good movie on Channel 13, Philip kissed her goodnight and let her go home to her own bed.

* * *

126

"So I won't be able to do your movie. I'm sorry, but it won't be difficult to find someone else. Of course, I'll stay until you do."

"When will you get married?"

"As soon as the divorce is through. Sandy'll be back in a day or two."

"Listen, don't do it. You want to get married? I'll marry you."

"What?"

"Don't marry that shmuck. You want to get married, marry me."

"But . . ." This was impossible. "But, you don't love me."

"How do you know?" But it was said lightly.

Diane's main emotion was one of embarrassment, and she was ashamed of it. Actually Mitch was a much better bet. A kinder, gentler, funnier man. But she loved Philip, even though she had no illusions about his character.

"Does he?"

"Of course."

Mitch's turn to remain silent. He contented himself with raising his eyebrows expressively.

"Anyway, I love him. That's the point."

And now Mitch was looking embarrassed. But unlike Diane, he had the courage to blunder on.

"Why's he marrying you?"

"Because he . . ." Diane caught herself before she said "he loves me" and substituted "because he wants to."

He'd said he loved her. But she'd put him in a position where, if he wanted her to stay around full time, to make his life tidy, to bring up Tania, he had to say it. He might be lying. But then again, he might not. The thought of it took her breath away.

"Do you know what makes me mad? Really mad?"

Sandy's question was gently put, but the possibilities of the answer raced through Diane's mind. That I'm going to marry

127

your husband? That your lover is, at first glance, an out-and-out con man? That your daughter probably thinks I'm her mother?

"What?"

"That they call it a pound of caviar, and it's really fourteen ounces. I wouldn't mind paying one-seventh more, but I really resent not getting the full amount. Not that I've ever actually paid for it myself, of course."

Diane smiled, said nothing. She thought, and suspected Sandy did also, that in a way Sandy had paid.

Sandy seemed to have suddenly grown up. She looked five years older and infinitely more beautiful. No longer a pretty young girl, now a woman with a dramatically tragic look all of her own.

"Philip wants to see you."

"Oh, dear. Why, do you know?"

"Not really, but I think it might be about a divorce."

"Yes, of course. We should get that cleared up while I'm here. I'll give him a call. He's not going to be all bitter and emotional about it, is he?"

"I don't think so."

"Restrained and heartbroken?"

"He seems to be bearing up quite well."

Diane tried to restrain her annoyance at Sandy's rather conceited assumption that her estranged husband should still be pining for her. Worse, it would never occur to her that Diane's constant presence in his house might be of interest to Philip. But, to be fair, why should it? Sandy knew that Philip had not found Diane attractive in the past, why should he now? She wondered if Sandy knew that she'd slept with Philip. Impossible to ask. And he was unlikely to have invited trouble by telling her. But maybe.

"Ever see Mom?" Sandy asked.

128

"Mom?"

"Mom. Surely you haven't forgotten Dennis's blue-haired Mom?"

"No, why should I?"

"We had lunch yesterday. She's in great form. Planning to have her face lifted and her swimming pool remodeled."

"But surely . . . are you guys on good terms?"

"Oh, yes. I didn't see her when I was married to Philip, but when I came back this time I found I rather missed her. We used to have a lot of fun together. So we had lunch. She gave me this scarf, do you like it?"

It seemed no one could stay angry with Sandy for long. Next thing she'd be having cozy little dinners with Dennis and Philip.

Philip appeared to be more shaken by his meeting with Sandy than he let on, or than Diane had expected him to be.

"It's all settled, my lawyer's going to draw up a separation agreement."

"And Tania?"

"We agreed she'd live with me. Alexandra will have whatever visiting rights she wants. Seems more sensible, until she gets settled in a place of her own."

"I see." Diane guessed there had rarely been a less contested custody battle.

"If you have a moment this afternoon, you might write to the credit card people and cancel her cards and charges. I don't see why this fellow—John, or whatever he's called–shouldn't pay her bills."

He went upstairs to his room. Diane watched him go, thinking that the transition from secretary to fiancée wasn't moving quite as quickly as she might have wished. She hadn't really expected him to rush in the door, take her in his arms, twirl her around and announce that nothing now stood in the way of their happiness. But even so.

She wondered if Philip had told Sandy they were getting married. She was sure he hadn't, and also sure that if she asked him, he'd look her straight in the eye and say he hadn't because he didn't want to give Sandy any leverage in the divorce.

Not asking those questions, and doing secretarial chores were all part of being a good wife. And Diane was determined to be an excellent wife. She would make Philip's life so comfortable, so smoothly organized that he would never regret having married her. She would be economical, efficient, undemanding, tactful, supportive and all the things Sandy hadn't been. She would care for his child, cook his meals, type his manuscripts and never sulk. Fidelity, of course, went without saying.

Which reminded her. David, who had been in California for a couple of weeks, should be back by now. She hoped he'd call and looked forward to explaining to him that she was now engaged and wouldn't be able to see him again. It would be the first time in her life she'd ever left a man, and she wanted to do it right. But he hadn't called. In fact, Diane had been the one who usually made the calls and that made her feel even more like making it clear that she was the one who was leaving. It seemed to her that she'd never been on equal terms with a man in her whole life. Father, teachers, employers, lovers, she'd always been the one trying to please, the one who loved, the one who feared disapproval and abandonment. And now with her husband, as he soon would be, the pattern held. Even when Philip said he loved her, she felt she's cornered him into it. And if he did, she certainly loved him more. Once again she was about to give a great deal of herself in return for a very small portion of the man involved. But she'd made a kind of unspoken bargain with Philip, and she intended to keep it.

She went into the office and dialed David's number. After a few rings he answered.

"Yeah." Half asleep and not much wanting to talk anyway.

"David, it's Diane." That sounded ridiculous, if he didn't recognize her voice, the call was pointless.

"Hi."

She could have thought of better lead-ins than that, but she soldiered on.

"Listen, I'm getting married."

"Whadda you mean?" Still not very interested.

"I'm engaged. Getting married. Quite soon; he's just waiting for the divorce to become final."

"Hey, that's wonderful, congratulations."

"Thank you. So, I can't go on seeing you and er . . ."

"No problem. I'm going to London end of the week anyway."

"Oh."

"Send it to the Plaza Hotel, please."

"Certainly, madam. Cash or charge?"

"Charge."

Sandy slid across her charge plate, and went to inspect a little basket on the counter full of little frilly nothings. A chorus-girl garter in red and black, some almost nonexistent panties. She chose one or two things to add to her order, and handed them across to the saleslady as she returned.

"I'm sorry, Mrs. Hope, but I'm afraid there's been some mistake. This charge plate's been canceled."

"Oh . . . Oh, yes, how silly of me. I'll pay cash."

Sandy opened her purse. She did, in fact, have just enough to pay for the nightdress, but in a rare moment of caution, decided not to. It would leave her with no money at all.

"I'm afraid I don't have quite enough with me. I'll come back for it later."

Slightly pink, more outraged than embarrassed, Sandy left the department, and took an elevator to the ground floor.

An hour later and after some tricky telephone calls, Sandy realized that she had only one credit card left. She could charge gas if she wanted to, but she didn't have a car. John always hired a limousine as soon as they got to any city. Still, she tucked it away in her purse, just in case. Disgusted, she threw her other charge plates into the wastebasket. How could Philip be so petty, so mean. She felt dejected and humiliated. She hoped Philip would never know she had tried to use the Bendel's charge, she hoped he thought she'd thrown them all away out of pride before she left home.

Fortunately, later that afternoon on the way to the hairdressers, she saw an almost identical nightdress in one of the hotel boutiques. It cost a little more, but really was rather better quality. She charged it to her room number and started to feel better almost immediately.

"Alexis."

"Just a minute." She turned off the faucet and called back through the open door. "Yes, darling?"

"Can you hear me?"

"Yes," but only just. He was calling to her from a matching bathroom, the other side of the bedroom. "What is it?"

She raised a foot through the bubbles, looked at it for a moment. Time for a pedicure, but maybe she'd last another day if she just touched up the big toe. She didn't even notice the short silence before he started again.

"Look. We've had a good time together, haven't we? It's been fun."

"Of course, sweetie."

"But things are different now. You can see that."

"Different?"

"Yes. Things change, nobody's at fault. And we've both got our own lives to live."

"Yes?"

"You didn't think the holiday was going to last forever, did you?" God, she was dumb. She wasn't even smart enough to be making this hard for him. She just didn't seem to understand. God knows he preferred stupid women, if only they wouldn't make him feel so fucking awful, for a minute, when he gave them their marching orders. So goddamn helpless. "I mean the hotel living and everything. You knew it was just for as long as it was fun."

Sandy felt a cold lump form in her tummy. She wanted to get out of the bath, partly to rush in and hug him, assure him everything was going to be all right, that she'd be better, prettier, sexier, happier. Just have him tell her what he wanted and she'd be it. Partly also because she'd feel better continuing this conversation on dry land. But although John liked their conversations through open matching bathroom doors, she'd noticed he didn't like to be followed into the bathroom. Where he spent an inordinate amount of time, emerging more handsome than ever. She lay in the now cooling water and waited for the death blow.

"But I thought we were getting married . . ." She abandoned all pride, knowing the situation was not salvageable.

"Now, darling, you know I'm married. Carrie would never give me a divorce. She's a good girl in her way, and very understanding."

Sandy knew then he was returning to his wife. Who was, as he said, understanding, and for all she knew a "good girl," though rather older then Sandy. And unarguably richer. Money, dammit, and she had none. What the hell was she going to do? It'd been some time since she'd seen any cash larger than a five dollar bill.

"You want me to move out?" her voice sounded very small, and little-girl-like, but she couldn't help it.

"Of course not, the suite's paid for until the end of the week, so you can stay here until you find somewhere else."

"But . . ." Sandy said, then started to cry.

Her words were lost to John, who had turned on the hot water.

"Another bottle of champagne," Sandy said. "Don't you think?"

"I don't know. I mean, isn't it just the tiniest bit extravagant?"

"That's the point. I have the suite—ghastly vulgar American expression—for another three days. John never spares any expense on himself. Why should I be any different?"

"Won't he mind?"

"Who gives a shit? I don't quite know who pays for it all, but it's too late to worry about that now."

"Well, in that case—and maybe another ginger ale for Tania. Why shouldn't she benefit as well?"

"Actually he's got off very light, no fault of mine. I went to Crouch and Fitzgerald and ordered some new luggage—I mean I can't leave here looking like a shopping-bag lady—charged it to the hotel, but they said no. So either John's given some small-minded instructions or they're getting wise downstairs."

"But you can still go mad with room service?"

"Sure. At least I think so. I mean, ordering the best champagne's a way of taking the temperature. What would you think about half a pound of caviar?"

134

"Better not, they might think you were teasing them."

"Perhaps you're right. They're not as naive as you might think." Diane had never, in fact, thought of the management of this hotel as naive. "I got a horrid letter from them this morning. Reminding me the suite was only booked until the end of the week and that they had a reservation for it on Monday. Imagine the nerve."

"Hm."

"I don't know what to do. John left me with two hundred dollars. Obviously most of that's gone already. What am I going to do?"

Diane considered the question. Or rather, questions. Why was Sandy's last two hundred obviously almost gone? What was Diane to do about Sandy? For she had no illusions about who would be left holding the baby, not necessarily Tania.

"How's Philip?"

"He's fine. Hard at work."

"I suppose he still wants this stupid divorce. I mean it hardly seems worth the trouble now."

"He seems to."

"Why? It isn't as though he wants to marry anyone else."

"Well . . ."

"He does? Who?"

"Well, actually . . . me."

Diane watched a variety of emotions cross Sandy's face. Surprise, frustration, disapproval, then a forced smile.

"Oh, God . . . Congratulations, Diane. Are you sure?"

Diane realized that, though she'd expected no enthusiasm from Claire or Mitch, she'd hoped for a better reaction from Sandy, which was, of course, ridiculous. She also remembered that it was the groom you were supposed to congratulate. The bride was supposed to be wished every happiness.

135

"What a beautiful little girl! Is she yours?"

Diane was completely thrown by the question. First of all, she herself always assumed that any adult female, not in uniform and the same color as the child she was accompanying, was its mother. What telltale, giveaway sign was she carrying around that made this park mother ask the question?

She was also thrown by what answer she should give. She could say: "No, she's my stepdaughter," or "She's the daughter of a friend," or "I work for her father." All of which would be sort of true, but she found herself unable to give any of these answers, imagining Tania listening and wondering. She smiled and opened her mouth a couple of times and then closed it. The woman looked at her curiously.

"Diane's my friend," Tania said, solving the problem neatly with two-year-old logic.

Diane hoisted Tania up onto the swing, and started to push her. She felt slightly sad about only being Tania's friend, in fairness she should have been her mother. But when she thought about it, the word "mother" to Tania probably only meant that pretty friend of Diane's who they visited occasionally.

"I'm afraid I can't afford champagne this time. My standard of living seems to have deteriorated in the past two weeks. But if you put enough ice in this, it's almost drinkable."

"I'm amazed you're still here. Have you made up with John?"

"That rat. Do you know I haven't heard a word from him since he moved out. I just got this little room until I find an apartment."

"Who's paying for it?"

"I am. Actually, I suppose Mom is. We had lunch the other day. She couldn't have been sweeter. If it wasn't for bloody Dennis I suppose I could have moved back in there. What a lot of burned bridges behind me. No going back."

There was just the hint of a question behind "no going back." Could Sandy be wondering if she could move back in with her and Claire, or perhaps with her and Philip, or maybe just with Philip?

"Onward and upward," Diane said briskly. "What're your plans?"

"I've got to find a place to live and a job. I'd better speak to Philip about money. I'm broke and, after all, he is my husband. Just."

"Don't let him know you're living here. It's the most expensive hotel in town."

"I had no choice. Apartments are hard to find and I don't really have enough money for a deposit until I find a job."

"How about a cheaper hotel?"

"Oh, darling, it's just for a few days. Until I find somewhere else."

"Till death us do part," Diane said, but silently, to herself. That was what you were supposed to say. In a real wedding. Though she could think of things that could part them sooner than that. Like Sandy and the expression on Philip's face as they walked down the aisle. Not the aisle literally, since as the third Mrs. Hope, all she seemed to deserve was this depressing room in City Hall. So much for childhood fantasies. Clouds of white tulle—tulle? Diane wasn't very good at fabrics, but tulle sounded right, or was it muslin? Mimosa, freesia, orange blossom—but maybe mimosa was orange blossom. And the music, another area where she seemed vague, but she'd know it if she heard it. The bridegroom, always faceless, but tall, undoubtedly good-looking and, of course, passionately in love. With her. The bridesmaids, without being quite as beautiful as she—radiant, yes, radiance would cover that problem—would be pretty, and their dresses, designed by her during adolescence in study hall, as was her wedding dress, would be really lovely. The guests would be elegant and distinguished, and the whole thing would be crammed into a miraculously transformed parish church, which for once would not be cold, damp, with laurels dripping outside, smelling faintly of cat.

Well, that part of the fantasy matched reality. The room was hot and stuffy, the fluorescent lighting harsh overhead and the faint smell was of diesel fumes from the street outside. This, she thought, was as far from home as she'd ever been.

"You may kiss the bride."

She stopped dreaming; Philip was looking at her. After a moment's hesitation, he kissed her. Everything seemed a little better, she wanted to cling to him, to be reassured, but remembered her audience. He released her, they turned, accepted congratulations, handshakes, kisses. Diane looked around. Claire, a little apart from the others, failed to meet her eye. Philip's parents, old and confused, wanting to accept her, but aware they'd sat through this same ceremony before and not understanding why Philip should be marrying this difficult, reserved woman when they'd all adored pretty little Sandy. Tania, solemn and interested, held by a new housekeeper, who regarded the whole proceedings with open-mouthed curiosity and suspicion. Billy, Philip's agent, whom she hardly knew. Most of their contact had been over the telephone, on business, when she'd been Philip's secretary. She knew he'd been charmed and delighted by Sandy. His look was not unkind, but not encouraging, either. She really had no one to represent her. Even Mitch had made an excuse, though he'd sent a generous present.

Diane realized she'd have given a great deal to have had Sandy at her wedding. To make it light and happy and glamorous. To make it work, to make it feel like a celebration.

"I don't suppose you'd want me to do your house over for you? Would you?"

"I don't think it would work, but thank you, darling. I'm sort of used to it the way it is, and anyway, it's all your own decor already."

Diane thought of the agonizing months she'd spent watching Sandy's mark being stamped on Philip's house, taking every change personally, resenting every pillow and flower vase. Now she liked it as it was, and felt grateful no one expected her to drag around department stores looking at fabric. Nothing, she reflected, not for the first time, works out quite as you expect it to.

"I just wondered. I've got to find work and I don't know how to start except with the people I know. Mom's given me a commission—I'm going to redo her pool house. All green and white."

"Good. I'm glad. Listen, if I hear of anything I'll let you know."

"How's Philip?"

"Fine."

Neither met the other's eye. Hard to go further. Diane, ostensibly still on her honeymoon. Sandy remembering.

"And the little person?"

"Angelic."

"Odd to think of you as stepmother to my baby. Funny the way things turn out."

For a moment Sandy looked beaten. And Diane was for the first time aware that a certain amount of courage went into being as frivolous as Sandy appeared to be.

"I suppose you'd think I was jealous if I said I was sorry you'd married him?"

"No."

Now they did meet each other's eye.

"You do love him, don't you?"

"Yes."

"You always did. I suppose I kind of knew it. In the back of my mind, never actually saying it to myself, you know what I mean?"

"Yes."

"But I never took it seriously. I mean, I knew what he was like."

"You married him."

"I did, didn't I? I suppose I just didn't think it would really count. I mean if I hadn't met him I was all lined up to marry Dennis. And now you've got my husband and my daughter."

"By default."

"By default."

A long silence.

"Mitch said he'd buy me lunch. Want to come along?"

"Oooo, I'd love it. If you're sure it's all right. Where?"

"Oh, somewhere frightfully grand, I'm sure. He can't afford to be seen anywhere else these days."

Diane sat in front of the mirror on her dressing table, brushing her hair. Fifty each side, then starting again. Philip lay on the bed, reading a magazine. Both half listened, quarter watched, a late-night movie on television. It seemed to her they had been frozen there, silent, unable to move for a long time. Then a commercial break. Once again, Diane wondered why the authorities thought that someone who was sitting up watching television at two-thirty in the morning would be a suitable person to adopt a retarded child.

"Don't you have a meat thermometer?" Philip asked.

"Yes."

"The beef was overdone."

140

"I know. You said. The Jacobsons were late."

"You should have turned the oven down."

"I did, but it was too late. And I misjudged it. I'm sorry."

The commercial switched to one advertising a Caribbean holiday. A nubile native girl with a large flower behind her ear, and a much smaller bikini. Philip's attention went back to the television. Diane glanced at him and at the television, drew in two deep breaths and started to brush her hair again. All right, the beef had been overdone, a pale pink instead of the deep red Philip liked. It hadn't been burned to a cinder, as his tone implied. And the soufflé had been perfect and the soup homemade, and she'd worn a becoming dress and done her hair well, and been polite to all the guests, and cleaned up afterward. None of which Philip thought worth mentioning. Diane felt tears of rage and disappointment rising to her eyes and tried to stifle them. She supposed what she was meant to do now was to discuss the problem, admit her fault, point out how well it had all gone and say he was being unfair. Or, alternatively, throw her hairbrush at him and express her anger. Or remain a doormat, and strive for such perfection that he would never be able to criticize her again. But none of these courses of action would have worked, because what Philip was saying was unanswerable, and in code. "Don't you have a meat thermometer?" meant "I don't like you. I don't want to live with you and be around you. I don't like being married to you. I don't particularly like being somewhere with people I don't know very well and be identified as your husband. I don't want to make love to you. I don't want to sleep in the same bed as you. I don't want to wake up beside you tomorrow morning. I don't want you, day after day, attached to me like a leech. I'm trapped."

Given a choice between a coded message and these words spoken out loud, Diane preferred the code.

"I'm going to check on Tania," she said.

She knew, and Philip knew, that Tania slept soundly through the night. But he nodded and she left the room. A few minutes later she returned.

"She's a little restless, I'll sit with her for a while. Don't wait up for me, I might fall asleep in there."

" 'Do cats eat bats? Do cats eat bats?' and sometimes 'Do bats eat cats?' " Diane was reading to Tania.

"Like carry me upside down like a bat?"

"Yes."

"Do cats eat bats?"

"I imagine they would if they could get the bat to sit still for long enough."

Tania considered this for a short moment, then asked, "And do bats eat cats?"

"Not unless the cat is unusually small and the bat is a giant."

"Then what do bats eat?"

"I don't know. What do you think?"

"Worms," Tania said, without a moment's hesitation.

"Only flying worms."

Tania looked puzzled.

"Because bats can only fly if they drop first. That's why they hang upside down. So if they were on the ground eating worms, what would they do when they wanted to fly home?"

"Climb a tree."

And Tania screamed with triumphant laughter. After a while she repeated "climb a tree" and found it just as funny the second time around. Philip came in while they were both laughing, his face lighting up with pleasure. He loved Tania so deeply it was like a pain to him, but he never quite knew what to say or do with her, and playing or reading with her bored him after a few minutes. Sandy, he knew, had failed even more deeply. Her image of motherhood was a beautiful woman, hair up, dress faintly fin de siècle, smelling of lots of expensive perfume, wafting into the nursery and kissing her child good night. The child was then supposed to curl up and drop off into a happy sleep, dreaming of her exquisite mother. He sighed. Diane looked up quickly. He read her mind and hastened to reassure her.

"You're a wonderful mother," he said, and put his hand affectionately on her shoulder.

Diane smiled up at him, trying not to show how extreme her reaction was to his praise. Then Tania demanded that Diane continue with the story, and Philip said he had some work to do, and went out. Tania continued to chortle from time to time and chant "climb a tree," and Diane wondered if she might dare suggest to Philip that they have a child of their own. Maybe if things were still going well when he came back from his California trip.

It was just bad luck that Claire was the stewardess who served drinks to Philip and his girl on the New York—Los Angeles flight. She recognized him instantly, though he had no memory of ever having seen her. He just knew Diane had a friend named Claire, whom he was willing to believe had been at Sandy's Christmas party and at his wedding. And, of course, the uniform didn't help.

Claire thought about it for a long time before she told Diane. Claire knew that she would have wanted to be told. She also knew that Diane wouldn't have wanted to know. And if Diane had looked happy for anything more than a week or two after marrying Philip, she'd have kept silent.

Diane understood all this, but she never quite forgave her.

Sandy stood in the doorway of the bedroom, looking in. Given even a moderate sum of money it would be possible to make it halfway cheerful, but given a moderate sum of money she wouldn't live here. She sighed. It was one of the rare times she felt defeated. And cheated. For the first time in her life she knew she was qualified to do something and she wasn't going to get a chance to do it. Each time she'd wanted to embark on a new career there'd been someone—well, actually, there'd been a man—who would encourage her, introduce her to the right people, buy her a typewriter, camera or whatever. Even though she'd never followed through. Sandy was silly, but she wasn't entirely dumb. She knew she'd been playing at it. It was fun to call yourself a writer and buy a lot of expensive creamy paper and yellow legal pads and a bunch of Pentels and nice sharp pencils, but when it came to getting up in the morning and using some of the new paper, there was always something more pressing to do. Not necessarily more important. Very often it might be nothing more than having breakfast in bed with John, or shopping with Mom and then, of course, there'd been Tania. People to please. She'd been in the business of pleasing people. Her job had been looking pretty and being agreeable, and making everything comfortable and pleasant for those around her. Which was why, dammit, she'd make a good interior decorator. There'd been nothing wrong with Mom's pool house; she'd done a good job there. If only Mom had left her alone a little. At the end she'd sometimes felt as though she'd been paid to go shopping with Mom. And that had made her feel amateur. But the professional—by that she meant being employed by strangers—commissions had not materialized. She'd failed to get a foot in the door. And now, where she was living was so grim that no one seeing it would ever employ her. It wasn't fair.

The telephone rang, and Sandy picked up the receiver. During the time it took to answer it she ran through a short mental list of who it could be. Starting at the top, in order of preference, was John—not likely he'd call, but a spark of hope still lived in her.

Or Mom, with news of a possible job from someone who'd seen the pool house—again not probable, but the odds were considerably better. Next on the list, also pleasurable and in Sandy's experience not unlikely, was the Unknown Factor. Some man she'd just dimly remembered being introduced to who'd spent the intervening four days in concentrated detective work tracking down her telephone number. In the dramatic sense of Sandy's life he played the part of Fate intervening; in another sense, he came from left field. But every man in Sandy's life had been random, an Unknown Factor, a chance meeting, the romance enhanced by the series of coincidences necessary for them to have met at all.

As she raised the receiver to her ear, she was almost convinced that the phone call would be a moment when the pendulum would reverse its swing, that in a week or two the ghastly little apartment in which she was living would be no more than a faint memory, a slightly embellished story to keep a dinner party amused for five minutes. She'd be wearing something black, very light, the entire dress weighing about two ounces, and maybe even a new piece of jewelry, perhaps modestly designed, but large diamond earrings and . . .

On the other hand, and she almost put the receiver down as she thought of it, why should the telephone be good news? It could be the landlord. She had a nasty sneaking feeling that if she balanced her checkbook, which seemed a grim and probably fruitless exercise, she might have found there wasn't quite enough money there to cover the check she'd been bullied into writing. She couldn't be sure, it might be all right, but if she'd been one of her own creditors she'd have made a point of depositing the check as quickly as possible on the basis of first-come being maybe the only one served.

A couple of other equally embarrassing possibilities crossed her mind, but it was too late now.

"Hello," she said in a small voice.

"Sandy, it's me. Are you all right?" A familiar voice. Diane's. The relief of it not being an appalling disaster made up for it not being any great change for the better.

"Pretty well all right." Her voice was stronger now, though she was shocked by having heard the panic in it.

"Look, I just heard of a job. Not exactly what I would have thought of, but it might suit you. Just a temporary thing."

"You have? What? How?"

"Well, actually, it was Claire's idea . . ."

"Oh."

With a wealth of meaning. Diane knew she'd made a mistake, and continued with rather less assurance than before. Also, she suddenly remembered a previous almost identical conversation with Lloyd, her florist friend, who had never forgiven her.

"At a hotel. In a jewelry shop. They're looking for someone. I mean, I know it's not really your kind of thing, but it's not hard work and you get to meet a lot of people . . ."

Sandy knew exactly what she meant. It was a job which guaranteed introductions to large quantities of rich men who were in the habit of buying expensive presents for girls. And not worrying too much about the mark-up. After all, the investment which the purchase represented would be paid off within an hour or two. They weren't looking for financial appreciation when they made their choices. Actually, it wasn't such a bad idea. That is, if she'd thought of it herself, dropped the fact that she'd taken the job casually into conversation. A small joke, a little laugh, then if the whole thing didn't work out she could profess shock, to have been nothing worse than attractively naive. But to take it now, and to have that wretched Claire to know she had, made it impossible. What a pity.

"I don't think so, thank you, but do thank Claire for thinking of me." That tone of voice was always so much more effective a snub than mere rudeness could ever be. And Sandy was remembering the disastrous job Diane had fobbed her off with. That seedy florist. And Diane was now married to her husband. Imagine if she'd taken the job and Diane had told him. But now she rather wished Philip could know how grandly she'd rejected this ludicrous and insulting suggestion.

Diane's summing up of what was going on in Sandy's mind was almost entirely accurate. But she felt obliged to press on. She was really worried about Sandy, who seemed to have taken John's defection harder than Diane would have thought possible. And dealing with Sandy's problems was infinitely preferable to thinking about her own.

"I meant as a stopgap—not permanently."

"I know, darling, and it couldn't be kinder of you, but . . ." Sandy glanced around the apartment, reflecting once again that while she lived here there was no possibility of getting decorating work. And it wasn't as though she were saving a fortune living in this slum. Real estate seemed to be a seller's market. Someone must be making a fortune. "What I'd really decided to do was sell real estate."

"What's this?"

A rhetorical question. Claire would have said it was a lollipop, as any fucking idiot could see. Diane, however, didn't belong to the school of thought that believes offense is the best defense.

"I'm sorry, it must be Tania's."

"What's it doing here?"

Another rhetorical question. Sandy, who probably wouldn't have recognized it as one, and might have thought of it as a genuine desire for information, would have said, "The angel must have left it there."

Diane repeated, "I'm sorry."

"I don't see why she should always have to have something in her mouth while she watches television, which incidentally, is far too often. She's gradually destroying the entire house."

As sometimes happened, Diane felt as though she were Tania's mother, and Philip her stepfather. And she didn't feel like fighting.

"I'm sorry," she said again. "But children of her age have no . . . um . . . awareness of sticky fingers and lollipops. She'll soon grow out of it. It's one of the things you have to live with if you have a small child."

"Until she grows out of it you might try and keep Amy on her toes. There's been a clear set of Tania's fingerprints on the stair wall for nearly three weeks now."

Even this did not make Diane point out that Tania was his child, not hers. It would be too unfair to Tania, and not honest, since she never thought of her in those terms. Instead she said exactly what she was thinking.

"Why do you always attack me when you're feeling guilty?"

"What d'you mean?" Philip's heart might have skipped a beat, but his expression never faltered.

"Fingerprints on the stairs aren't an adequate reason for your having a girl friend."

"What the hell're you talking about?"

"You know what I mean."

"No, I don't."

Diane shrugged, she certainly wasn't about to start a rigmarole about "a friend of mine saw you on the plane" and then listen to "I just bumped into an old friend at the airport and we sat together" and the "that's not the way it looked to my friend" and so on. It would be too degrading for both of them.

"You've been acting strange ever since I got home."

"I think I've already explained the reason for that."

"Are you getting your period, or are you just going crazy?"

"Hi, David. It's Diane."

"Oh . . . hi . . ." Then a guarded silence. Still, having come so far, making this call, she went on. "Diane. You remember me? I'm damned if I'll go through that dance again."

David laughed.

"Oh, Diane. Sure. How are you?"

"Fine. I was just calling to . . ."

"Listen, honey, I'm in the middle of something right now. Why don't you come over tomorrow—no, call me. Tomorrow, about this time."

"I . . . David . . . sure. Okay."

And there she was. Twenty-four hours to change her mind. To get out of it. To justify it. Twenty-four hours to make up with Philip. If only he would talk to her. If only she could talk to him. And whatever her problems with Philip were, they weren't going to be solved by this. Tomorrow she just wouldn't call.

The next day, back from the hairdresser's and carrying a new dress in a shopping bag, Diane was sure she wouldn't call. She glanced at her newly painted nails as she picked up the receiver. David liked women to be little dolls, just as Sandy's John had. And at least partly because it kept them busy, or occupied, or content. Polishing nails, setting hair, making up their faces. Lacquer and lipstick, shoes and stockings, accessories and jewelry. God forbid sandals or jeans. Anything easy or natural was called unfeminine.

Maybe he wouldn't be there. That would be good, God would be taking the decision out of her hands. He'd have forgotten, or gone out and she'd have enough pride not to call again. Maybe.

"Oh, yeah. Diane," he yawned. "What time is it?"

"Twelve-thirty. Did I wake you?"

"No, yes. I was late last night."

"I'm sorry. I'll call back later."

"No, come on over. Give me half an hour."

David seemed to be completely awake, if a little puffy around the eyes, when he opened the door. Newly shaven, his hair still wet from the shower, slightly too much aftershave. He wore a terry-cloth robe, it felt warm and a little damp to Diane as he pulled her into a hug.

"I'm on the phone. Come on in."

She followed him into the bedroom. He lay back on the bed, on top of the covers. The bed was pulled up, but not made. Diane perched on the end. Her new dress felt wrong. She'd bought it for sitting in the other room. For looking elegant and unobtainable. At least for starters.

David picked up the telephone, which was laying off the hook on the night table.

"Yeah, I'm back." He listened to something on the other end of the line, glanced at Diane, covered the phone with his hand and said:

"Get undressed."

Diane stood up, started to unbutton her dress, knowing she was doomed to react to that peremptory order with a hundred times more sexual excitement than the average girl did to champagne, night clubs, orchids and whatever else Barbara Cartland had taught her was romantic.

She undressed carefully, trying to show her body to its greatest advantage. David watched her, but continued his telephone conversation quite competently. At last she stood naked.

"Swiss francs or marks? " David said, untying the belt of his robe.

Diane crept up the bed, opened his robe, and lay against his body, trembling, almost sobbing, as he wound up his deal on the telephone.

If it took her so much time and trouble to stay reasonably in shape, how did a man who gambled all night, who never seemed to go outdoors, stay in such perfect shape? A flat, muscular stomach and a suntan. Maybe just incessant fucking. But surely that wouldn't give him a perfect tan.

* * *

"Hello, sweetie. Where've you been?"

Double surprise. First, Philip's enthusiastic greeting, and then, his showing enough interest in her to have noticed she was late.

"Oh, shopping. Odds and ends."

"Good news. Billy just called, I've sold the first serial rights for *Something Borrowed* to *Esquire*. Get changed and let's go out and celebrate."

Diane's immediate reaction was one of delight. *Something Borrowed* was a manuscript she'd lived with. She'd typed it and retyped it countless times; she knew whole passages by heart. It was a moment she could appreciate, one that would have been lost on Sandy. And she was aware that Philip knew it. His smile of pleasure also contained some gratitude. For caring about his book, but more for never referring to the girl he'd taken to California. He knew that Diane knew about her, but it had never been mentioned again. Her silence, he assumed, being part of the unspoken agreement, the compromise on which their marriage was founded. She must know that his feelings for her were less than passionate, less than entirely sexual. And he knew it must be painful to her. It wasn't her fault that he desired Sandy and girls like her. But it wasn't his fault, either.

Diane hugged him. If only the sale had been made yesterday, and Philip had been like this, then maybe this afternoon would never have happened. And thinking this, she hoped he wasn't as aware as she was that, despite a bath at David's apartment, her hair smelled of sex and aftershave.

Chapter Eight

"I love it. I wouldn't change anything about him for worlds. I love his ghastly clothes . . ." Diane rattled on, not really expecting approval or sympathy from Claire, but carried away by her woman's instinct to discuss her lover with any audience she could get to sit still for it. "I love his ties which look as though he'd just come back from one of your less distinguished racetracks. I love it that he sings in the bath and while he's getting dressed, and knows the words to the most dreadful songs. That he wears a big gold ring on his little finger."

"Well, that makes it all very clear. Now how about casting the same amount of light on the invisible charms of whatshisname—your and her mutual husband."

"I'm not entirely sure that's what mutual . . ."

"I'm not entirely sure that's what husband means."

Diane sighed, ready to dig in and try and defend herself, and Philip, and Sandy. Knowing she was wasting her breath.

"I know Philip's real and David's just self-destruction and high-powered sex, but I can't help myself."

"Just don't go falling in love with him, though I'm not sure he's not a better bet than the one you married. But you *are* married. *And* there's Tania."

"I won't." And as Claire looked at her skeptically, "I won't, really. Promise."

Love didn't really come into it; it was more like an obsession.

Very soon Diane realized that each time she and David went to bed they had to go a little further. That when they came to a full stop they would end. And since there are not infinite possibilities in lovemaking, she tried to add something each time, but not to use up all her ammunition at once. She also realized that he loved to hear stories of her past. She took to wearing more conservative, almost matronly clothes on the days she planned to tell him something which would be of prurient interest to him. She had realized right at the start that she wasn't qualified to compete on a tarty, sexy level. She wasn't young enough or pretty enough to entice him with low-cut dresses or tight shirts, and besides, what had drawn him to her in the first place was what he thought of as "class." What held him now was the contrast between her respectable appearance and her tales of exotic sex and degradation.

She would arrive at his apartment, and instead of kissing him hungrily, telling him she loved him, tearing off her clothes, begging him to hold her, she would give him a peck on the cheek, accept a drink and sit primly on a chair, legs neatly together, then tell some little anecdote, usually made up, of an incident which had taken place earlier in the day, while she was shopping at Saks, or lunching with a woman friend at a smart restaurant. Then gradually she would lead the conversation toward an incident in her past. Preferably one that had taken place before she came to America. She could tell he thought of Europe as definitely classy.

Despite David's conviction that a woman's place was in the beauty parlor, you could tell he was impressed by Oxford. So when Diane's modest claim to class in the sense of expensive labels and brand names was exhausted, she sometimes fell back on higher education. He wasted no time in wondering how she got there, or in being impressed by a series of scholarships. Instead he associated Oxford with her belonging to the type of "good family" who could afford Ivy League college fees.

Some reference to this now rather dim past led Diane to talk about George. She talked about her affair with him mainly to incite David's voyeuristic passion, but also, on a lesser level, from a need to talk about him. Harder to find that ear than one might imagine. From Claire, she would get a sort of contempt followed by an obscene sarcasm designed to nip in the bud any signs of self-pity, introspection or other forms of random, over-the-shoulder, looking back. No Lot's wife she. Sandy? Hard to discuss life in the gutter with a butterfly whose own existence had been only a series of wheatfields spotted with cornflowers and poppies. Philip? For obvious reasons they kept references to each other's sexual past to a minimum. Mitch, oddly enough, would have listened and understood, but that would have left him with an opening to indulge in a "just between us two losers" equal-time bargain. David was perfect: he listened with enthusiasm to the surface sexual content; heard, but ignored, the subtext.

George. Twelve years later he could still make her stomach turn over. A turn of phrase or the smile of a stranger would bring back some forgotten incident. She would remember something he'd said, and carry the phrase with her all day until she wore it out.

"He was a clever but lazy undergraduate," she told David, "and a rich, spoiled, good-looking prick. He was twenty-three, he hadn't come up to Oxford directly from school and he seemed as though he were just visiting. In fact, he spent a lot of his time in

154

London. He wanted to be friends and, almost as an afterthought, absentmindedly, took me to bed. Afterward, he thought—he hoped—I'd laugh it off, but it was too late. I was in love. We tried: he tried to be my friend; I tried to be his lover. He wanted me to be the girl he had lunch with on Sundays. I wanted to be the girl he spent the previous night with and who was going to spend Sunday afternoon in his bed. But I was passive and self-controlled. I might show myself hurt and disappointed, but I never made a scene and there were parts of his life I fitted into more neatly than his latest debutante. Then, I'm still not quite sure why, he asked me to come with him to Italy for ten days. During the Long Vac. I had arranged a summer job, but I didn't say anything to my employer. I quit at short notice, lied to my parents, spent the money I'd earned on clothes and set off for Italy. When I got there I found it wasn't just the two of us. A friend of his from London, Tom, whom I'd met and quite liked, was already there. Tom was nothing like as attractive as George, but even so he had his share of girls. The third or fourth day, one of these girls—I think her name was Pamela—arrived. She was a model, from London. I was scared and jealous. I thought George would find her more attractive than I. I imagined he would either take her from his friend, which wasn't likely, or more probably resent being stuck with the plain girl while his friend got the beauty. The first lunch he paid quite a lot of attention to her. Nothing beyond the bounds of good manners, but I felt like the Little Mermaid."

"The little what?"

"The Little Mermaid. As though I were walking on swords. That statue in Copenhagen? Hans Christian Andersen? Danny Kaye?"

Sometimes talking to David was disconcertingly like talking to Claire. "I mean, I was jealous. But that afternoon she sat out in the sun. I should have said before—she had long red hair and

155

white skin. By drinks time she was scarlet and blotchy. I was beside myself with joy. And then she kept George—all of us—waiting for an hour while she painted over her sunburn. After that George never paid her any more attention than was necessary not to insult Tom. And even Tom seemed faintly relieved when he took her to the airport a couple of days later. She had a commercial or something, but even so it made me feel good to be there for the whole vacation while she was just there for a long weekend.

"But then George said at lunch he had to go back to London for a day and a half. Leaving the next afternoon. It was the day before we were supposed to go on to Venice."

Venice, Diane thought. Venice. I might as well be talking about Detroit. George and I might as well have enrolled at the University of Miami, the way I tell it, or the way David's imagination fills in the gaps. But I'm the one who skipped the descriptions of hawthorn in Hardy. He's never heard of Hardy. Philip has but we'd never talk about him. And he'd just be bored if I describe the figs, the prosciutto, the terra-cotta, the dry heat of the sun, or the brown hard muscles on George's arm.

"I didn't know what to say. 'Of course, I'll go back with you, it's fine.' Because, of course, it wasn't. I didn't expect my lovely holiday to be cut short and I was disappointed. Also, if I went home now I'd have to go to Ireland and face a certain amount of third degree about why I'd quit my job and where I'd been and with whom. Of course, even if I didn't go home I'd be asked the same questions, but by mail. I could take weeks to answer and ignore the more inconvenient ones. But George had paid my fare. I could hardly expect him to take me back to London and then back again to Venice and I didn't have enough money to volunteer to pay for the trip. Then George said, casually: 'Why don't you and Tom go on to Venice? I'll meet you there.' I was relieved and happy. We drank another bottle of wine. George and I went to bed. It was even better than usual. I slept afterward and woke at about six. Later we went to Tom's room for a drink. He had the English papers and we were leafing through them, sipping Campari when Tom's phone call came through. He was making travel arrangements. I didn't pay much attention beyond thinking maybe I should have made the call. I'd slipped into packing for both men, dealing with hotels and other kinds of housewifely duties. I heard him book a room for two in a hotel in a little town on the way to Venice.

"I didn't move. I waited; George said nothing. Maybe he hadn't heard. Surely yesterday's *Times* couldn't be that fascinating. I didn't look at him. He turned a page. Tom put the phone down.

" 'Do you think a half portion of pesto would be a mistake before the cappelletti?' he asked.

" 'Not if we walked to the restaurant. Actually, that little café's on the way. We might stop for a drink.' George said.

"I knew if I said nothing in a moment it would be too late. But I was confused. If Tom intended seduction, a double room wasn't essential and also would he have booked it in front of his friend? No, doing it so openly showed it was innocent. I was just being silly. After all, we were students, traveling on summer vacation. We weren't exactly hitchhiking but a certain amount of roughing it seemed appropriate. I suppose I could have said, 'I'd prefer my own room. I'll pay for it myself. I've got enough money, I think.' But I didn't. The same way I wasn't sure whether George had said anything to Tom about paying for me during the next two days. Money can be very embarrassing at times. And Tom seemed stuck with me. What if he'd wanted to spend the time some other way? Picking up a girl, for instance. I said nothing, and my smile said I didn't want to be any trouble. I was fairly silent during dinner. Later, in bed, I said: 'Are you sure it wouldn't be a better idea for me to come back to London with you?' George seemed surprised. 'Of course not. Don't you want to see Venice? Unless you've something you'd rather do in London.' His tone was dismissive, the subject not interesting and now closed. So the next day I packed his bags, we had lunch and went to the airport. His flight was a little late. We had drinks in the bar and ran out of conversation, the way you do at an airport. Eventually his flight was called, and Tom and I were left alone. I was nervous—not sexually nervous—but unsure of myself. Worried about being a bore. Maybe the uneasy conversation at the airport bar would be the high point of our communication in the next two days. We took a taxi back into town. At the hotel he yawned and said: 'Well, I'm for a little nap. Meet you in the bar about seven-thirty?' It was quite reassuring; at least he wasn't going to abandon me. I wasn't sleepy, but I didn't feel like going sightseeing by myself. I used the time to wash my hair and give myself a manicure and pedicure. Afterward I read a bad detective story. It seemed like a waste of a day in Rome. Drinks and dinner were pleasant enough, though I wasn't sure we'd have much left to say to one another by the time we got to Venice. We went to see an American movie dubbed into Italian. Again, not thrilling, but okay. Back at the hotel, Tom kissed me good night on the forehead, outside my bedroom door. I was so relieved I could have hugged him, but that might have defeated its own purpose. I went to bed feeling safer but missing George.

"I packed for Tom the next day; he was pleased and grateful, which made me happy. Approbation. He settled the hotel bill; I assumed he and George'd made some arrangement about that. We picked up our rented car and drove away."

A moment of silence. Diane began to feel sorry she'd started. She seemed to have gotten into a very long story which she'd have trouble getting out of. She'd a feeling this time David would say, "That's all?" And, of course, it wasn't. What the hell had she

158

thought was going to happen between Rome and Venice? She stalled for time, treating David to a couple of architectural descriptions, a menu from a rural inn. He lighted a cigarette and his eyes assumed a faraway look. He was bored.

"When we'd checked into hotels before, of course, I'd been with George and I was proud that whoever it was knew that this man was my lover. Now I desperately sought around in my mind for some phrase to show that Tom and I were just friends, sharing a room to save money.

"We were silent on the way up. The porter put down our cases, showed how the primitive phone system worked and, with a flourish of pride, disclosed a refrigerator full of drinks. You know the kind, looks like your own home, with a little inventory in the inside of the door. 'Good idea,' Tom said, 'I could use a drink. Open something.' I poured us both a stiff one. He might have been able to use a drink; I'd have killed for one. The porter lingered, was tipped, hovered, bowed and retreated. Leaving us alone. In my panic I'd toyed with the idea of offering him a drink. I took a large gulp of mine, Tom sipped his, put it down, started to unbutton his shirt. I stepped back, an involuntary, purely instinctive reaction. He appeared not to have noticed. 'I'm going to take a shower,' he said. 'Get into bed.' Without waiting for any reaction from me, he went into the bathroom, closing the door, but not locking it. After a moment I heard the pathetic trickle of a shower installed for American tourists without any concession to the lack of water pressure. I stood there for a moment, finished my drink."

This part was harder to explain, because there were several versions, all of them true. Like the *Alexandria Quartet*, she thought, but that wasn't quite it. That was four people telling the same story, each from his own point of view. And this story had never actually been told before. She had told it to herself, as though rehearsing the telling of it to another person. And each version she rehearsed was true, no fact changed. But she never ended up understanding clearly what exactly had happened.

"I considered my options. I could run out of the room, dash downstairs, and by the time Tom was dry and dressed, I could, in my nonexistent Italian, be appealing to the middle-aged woman behind the reception desk, the one who'd looked at my passport and then at me with such distaste. She already obviously considered me a whore. Would she really be sympathetic to my complaint that a man I'd just checked in with was making sexual advances? Probably not. Obviously I would have to face up to Tom. Sophisticated amusement seemed the most attractive course of action. Or tears and innocence. That would have worked better if I hadn't earlier been at some pains to demonstrate in a dozen fairly subtle ways that George and I were sexually active—a kind of misjudged showing-off, based only on my fear he would think me too unattractive to be his friend's lover and assume the relationship was what people used to call platonic. Right then it would have been all right with me if he'd thought me dowdy and plain to the extent of deformity. Or would it? Part of me was fascinated, almost charmed by his approach. Why should he be so sure, how could he be so arrogant and insulting if he didn't know, if he didn't recognize that part of me I kept so carefully hidden, especially from George? I felt he could explain some mystery about me, the clue to which I'd been looking for most of my adult life. It was as though he saw and wanted in me something George had never even suspected existed. How had he been so sure? From that question, that first feeling of curiosity about a man I'd never wondered about, had taken at face value, came the first twinge of desire. The guilt, anxiety and the thought of George left me as hopelessly committed to Tom as if I were already spread out, naked on the bed, with him inside me."

She mightn't be discovering anything new about herself with

this revelation, but David stubbed out his cigarette, shifted his position slightly on the bed. His attention was hers. This story, so painfully, so foolishly embarked on would be paid off. Soon.

"He came out of the bathroom, wearing nothing but a skimpy towel around his waist. I was standing where he'd last seen me. I might not have moved, except my glass was now full again. 'I thought I said get into bed,' he said. 'No,' was all I could whisper, though I knew I would obey. 'Now you've made your token protest, do as I tell you. Unless, of course, you want to be roughed up a bit—raped. But I don't see that in you.' I said nothing. 'Or do you? It's not an uninteresting idea.' 'No, please.' 'Why are you whispering? Are you afraid of me?' 'Yes, I am. I am afraid of you.' 'Good, but you want me, don't you?' Silence from me. 'It doesn't matter, you will.' He lay back on the bed. 'Undress.' I looked at him a moment, and almost despite myself started toward the bathroom. 'No.' I stopped. 'No, undress here. I want to watch.' I'd undressed in front of a man before, of course. Never with enormous confidence, though obviously I was younger then, and firmer and so forth. But I was being watched by a man whom I suddenly realized had never touched me. And I don't mean just sexually. Suddenly I was unable to remember even a time when he'd taken my hand to help me out of a car. It seemed completely possible that his skin had never touched mine, let alone a kiss, a held hand, some token of affection. In fact, I was chillingly aware that his behavior didn't necessarily guarantee sexual desire. It might just be part of some complicated and cruel game. Tom was famous for his unkind practical jokes. It was not a reassuring thought. 'I'm waiting,' he said, and I found myself starting to unbuckle a sandal. 'No, shoes last. Start with your shirt.' I slowly started to unbutton my shirt. It was the middle of summer, I wasn't wearing much. 'No, shoes last, I said.' So, I was there, naked except for a pair of high-heeled sandals, standing in front of someone I'd come to think of as a friend, but now

161

realized was a complete stranger. 'Good, now turn around slowly. Good, very nice. Now you may come here.'?"

Diane stopped, she was almost in tears, she looked at David with a silent appeal, she didn't want to go on.

"Don't tell me the rest, show me. No, go back a little, to where you were undressing."

Well, why had she told him the story anyway, except to get this reaction? She stood up and started to unbutton her shirt.

"What happened in the end?"

"Much the same as just happened now. It was much better with you, of course."

"I meant the next day. When your friend—George—came back?"

"Oh, nothing. It was all back to normal."

David grunted, yawned. He pulled the covers up and closed his eyes.

Nothing dramatic, in fact, had happened. There had been no yelling, no tears, no recriminations, no accusations, no remorse. But one or two smaller things had occurred. George came early from the airport, and found Diane in the bath. He leaned in, kissed her, took her out and made love to her, still damp, with more than his usual passion. He asked nothing, she volunteered nothing. She never knew whether her lover had set her up, or if she had been wantonly unfaithful to him. On the other hand, she never again went to bed with a man when she was completely sober.

Chapter Nine

Diane was a woman who would never in a million years dream of opening a letter addressed to anyone but herself. Which is as it should be. On the other hand, she was reasonably adept at reading upside down any correspondence left open on a desk. Who isn't? There is, she thought, left briefly alone in David's apartment, a very thin line between conventionally accepted human behavior and something really shameful.

What she was supposed to do was get dressed and get out. She wasn't in a hurry, though David apparently was. She'd got the afternoon free. For him. He'd managed to squeeze her in, scheduling their afternoon lovemaking with an efficiency a time and motion consultant might have applauded. Which left her high and depressed, satisfied and anxious, expertly loved and lonely. She didn't feel like taking a bath and a session of carefully redoing her hair and makeup, both essential if she were to return home looking the way she did when she left. It was only an hour or two since she'd done all that, with enthusiasm and pleasure, though mixed with anxiety since David was capable of casual last-minute cancellations and had been known not to show up. Anticipation, in the word of Carly Simon, made the difference. It was fun to dress to be undressed, boring to dress to go home to peel potatoes and spend an evening of sullen silence in front of the television set. Even if it was Channel 13. The ballet from Lincoln Center or *All in the Family*. What was the difference? Who gave a shit?

She put on David's robe, still damp and a little cold now, but smelling of his overpowering aftershave. If she'd never slept with him it would have been a subject for a joke, now it was the most erotic association she knew. For her, quite literally, it was the smell of sex. From nowhere she suddenly remembered seeing a man selling perfume on the street, yelling at passersby: "Why wander around this city smelling like a rancid beast? Buy . . ." And mentioning some surprisingly expensive brand of scent. It had made her smile for several blocks.

She passed a mirror and noticed that, contrary to what the movies and Madison Avenue tell us, women don't really look all that hot in men's bathrobes. She tightened the belt, and put her hands in the pockets, trying to add a little style to her reflection. Her fingers closed on a pack of cigarettes and a flexible circular object. She took the cigarettes out, started to open the pack before she realized they were menthol. David smoked Marlboros, so that was clear enough. Menthol had always seemed to Diane a woman's cigarette anyway. She looked at the other object she'd felt in the pocket, an elastic hairband. Immediately she had a mental picture: the girl, young, blonde, long hair, very slim, standing in David's bathroom, wearing his robe. On her, however, it wasn't lumpy, it emphasized her slimness. She had the band between her teeth as she twisted her hair up on top of her head before she got into the bath. Diane wandered into the bathroom, looked at the stuff on the shelves. The medicine cabinet would probably tell her all she wanted to know, but some remaining vestige of self-respect prevented her from opening it. Still, a logical mind could reconstruct much from the rows of bottles and containers on the window ledge. Even in this day of unisex products. Diane knew that it was not only possible but likely David used conditioner on his hair, but a brand for delicate or bleached hair probably wasn't his. Which meant there was a girl who was in a position to wash her hair in his bathroom. Not a drugstore brand either, but the kind expensive hairdressers hit you with while you're still reeling from the cost of the haircut. A neat little Identikit was being constructed. The girl at least moderately affluent, more than likely single. Married women tended to wash their hair at home, or the beauty parlor, rarely in men's apartments. The bottle was half empty. So unless she'd come over with a half-used bottle (which in itself suggested a suitcase or overnight bag), she was in the habit of sleepovers, hair-washing, general hanging out. Maybe she even kept clothes here. Diane hesitated by the door of the closet, put out a hand toward the knob. But she didn't open it. Snooping was unattractive, and did she really want to see a black nylon negligee hanging among David's too-tightly-cut suits? Instead, she passed on to the fat wad of hundred dollar bills. Diane was constantly amazed by how much money David casually carried around with him. It was as though he were, snail-like, carrying his assets on his person. His watch, his lighter, his ghastly gold ring, his cash in its heavy gold clip. She didn't get the impression that he did it in order to be able to make a quick getaway. More a matter of displaying his credentials.

Also on the table were a pack of Polaroid film and an out-of-focus photograph of a rather green David sipping a cup of coffee. Since he was wearing a bathrobe and reading the Sunday papers, she had to assume it was a morning-after happy snap. And Polaroids themselves had a definite sexual connotation.

The thought drew her eye, without hesitation, to the night tables which stood on either side of the huge bed. The one on David's side was a little open. Not left open, just not properly closed. Hating herself, Diane, without touching the drawer, but leaning over for a better angled view, looked in. There were the rest of the Polaroids, fortunately facedown. An open packet of amyl nitrates and the end of what was obviously a vibrator. New to Diane: she'd neither seen nor had any dealings with either. So, following the keen detective part of her mind, that meant . . . To hell with it, there were certain things better not dwelt on. She'd never imagined she was David's only woman, so what was the difference? Except Identikit details didn't help.

"I thought," said Diane, with a puzzled air, "a six hundred was one of the big ones."

"What?" Mitch sounded equally at sea.

"Your car, it says six hundred on the back. I thought that the six hundreds were sort of limousines. Is it custom-made or something?"

"Right."

"For you? That's very flashy."

"And the four-fifty SLC only has two doors."

"I think so. But why make a special six hundred that looks like a regular one?"

"Well, I bought it secondhand . . ."

"I still don't see."

". . . and I thought I'd jazz it up a little. Make it more powerful."

"You had the engine modified?—if that's the word."

"Na, what for? I'm not going to race it. What do I need with zooping it up? I just went to a junkyard and bought the little silver numbers off a wrecked Mercedes. You think I should change them back?"

"Well, maybe just to something a little more probable. What's the next step—fake Gucci loafers? An imitation Cartier watch?"

"You watch it, girl, when this deal's signed I'm going to buy a penthouse and give parties and guess who won't be asked if they don't show a little respect."

"Well, I hope you buy it from, or I suppose I should say, through, Sandy. She's got a job selling real estate."

"Selling real estate?"

"Well, she's got a job anyway. Like three-quarters of all urban women between the ages of thirty-five and fifty-five, she's gotten a divorce and taken a job in real estate. Apparently, though, there are some token qualifications required, not to mention working papers. So, as far as I can make out, she's a kind of apprentice. Makes coffee, runs errands, fills in. Once in a while she gets a little bonus, a kind of finder's fee if she brings some business their way. Otherwise it's not much. Still, she's stuck with it for more than a month."

"I suppose Philip gives her a little?"

"Yes."

"Not much though, I'll bet."

"I think they worked out something that's fair."

"Don't get snotty, I only asked. Poor kid. Why the hell don't you girls stay home? Bunch of wetbacks, all of you."

"Under our Shetland sweaters and neat tweed skirts?"

"Yeah."

"Call of the West, I expect. If I fuck up here—sorry," she interjected as Mitch flinched at the obscenity, "there's always a life for me in Japan. I'll be working in a sushi bar and Sandy will swan in, dripping in diamonds, and borrow ten yen off me."

"In the meantime, tell her she can introduce me to her boss, so she can maybe pick up a couple of bucks."

"She's working hard. She's taking her real-estate exams next month, so maybe she can actually sell you an apartment."

"Honey, I love you and I'm delighted to do anything within reason for your friend, but putting off buying an apartment doesn't come into that category."

"You mean you're really going to buy a place? Now?"

167

"A penthouse. A duplex penthouse. I just got through telling you."

"But you said when you'd got your deal signed."

"Yeah, this afternoon."

"Oh, I thought . . . You mean it's for real?"

"That's no way to talk to your former employer. Didn't you always get your paycheck—in the end?"

"I did. You mean, you really pulled it off?"

"Five pictures. Development guaranteed. Don't have to ask for approval under four and a half. All past misunderstandings forgotten."

"You're kidding."

"No, I'm not. It's the big time, baby."

"And why don't you go fuck yourself?"

Sandy was not normally foul-mouthed. In fact, like Mitch, she tended to wince at language that Claire and Diane thought nothing of using, but she hadn't actually said those words. Bad enough even to have thought them. What she did say was, "Certainly, I'd by happy to." She hoped that her ladylike smile and slightly emphasized English accent might make the point that it was hardly appropriate to ask someone of Sandy's caliber: "Why don't you pick up my dry cleaning on your way back *if* you *have to* go out for lunch?"

Going out for lunch wasn't something Sandy got to do very often. In theory there was a kind of roster for manning the telephones during the lunch break. In practice, rank and seniority were pulled, especially since the fully fledged realtor would waft out of the office, fanning a cloud of perfume with newly polished nails, jingling with gold chains and bracelets, calling over her shoulder, "Business lunch," or "Only time she could view that turkey we've been trying to unload on Park and Seventy-first." Invariably Sandy was left to answer the phones. Any attempt on her part to pretend that leaving the office between the hours of twelve-thirty and two was in the course of duty would have caused cross-examination unless, as was sometimes the case, she'd been sent out for sandwiches. The good bit was that she was alone in the office without that bevy of harpies. The bad part was that she bore alone the full brunt of seemingly automatic unpleasantness from each client who rang up. She sometimes wondered if real-estate women were so blood-curdlingly tough because the clients baited them, or if the clients were so awful because they knew it was the only way not to get bullied.

But today she'd said in a small, high voice, which to her sounded scared, that she hadn't had a lunch break all week, and it was Friday, and it was important, really. And so she was on her way out, almost lighthearted except for being humiliated by that bitch. No, she mustn't even think like this—first she'd think it and then she'd say it, and in no time she'd be like one of them.

The lunch wasn't important in the way she'd implied. It wasn't a doctor's appointment or a lunch with a rich single man, the kind of thing they'd understand. The need to stay healthy and to replace one's "ex" before the alimony payments petered out. But it was important to Sandy. She was going to see Mom. To gossip and chat in comfortable surroundings, to relax and be treated like the person she really was, not some kind of retarded underling. Especially since she mustn't look like a wet rag tonight.

"Nothing much," she said to Mom, gratefully sipping very cold white wine out of a sensuously large glass. "I'm going to rather an amusing dinner party tonight, but mostly I've been staying home. I'm studying for my real-estate exams." The second was not strictly true; in her heart Sandy knew she wouldn't last long in that bitch-eat-bitch business. Fortunately, and not surprisingly, Mom took her up on the party reference.

"Where?"

"Oh, the Cliffords. They were friends of John's and mine. More his, I'd always thought. But they asked me to dinner tonight, which was nice of them." Actually, they'd been old friends of John's and had, it seemed to Sandy, always been a trifle distant with her. But maybe she'd been mistaken. It was her they'd asked, and surely they—surely everyone—knew that he'd left her.

"You look so tired, you poor child. And so pale. Oh dear, I often wish that you and my Dennis had . . ."

"Mm." Sandy sighed. More and more frequently of late, she too wished she'd stayed put in Mom's comfortable house, waited on hand and foot, with no duties except looking pretty and being pleasant and going shopping. Maybe it wasn't too late.

"Of course, I'm very fond of Marcie, but all the same . . ."

"Marcie?"

"Dennis's fiancée. She's a sweet girl. Didn't you know?"

"No. How . . . where did he meet her?"

"On an airplane."

"A stewardess? Tell me more."

Some sense of slight curiosity and amusement saved Sandy from feeling that yet another door had been closed behind her. It was tough to keep leaving men and then find that they married someone else almost immediately, especially when she was alone and frightened. But Dennis marrying a stewardess. Well!

"I believe she had a job with an airline for a while. She's a very educated girl and comes from a good family."

Mom was putting her in her place. She'd better look out or that would be another door closed, if it wasn't already. Marcie must be getting the same treatment Sandy had. Lucky girl.

"I'm happy for him. She's a lucky girl."

Mom smiled, mollified.

"Tell me what you're going to wear tonight." A peace offering. Which probably meant that occasional lunches would continue.

170

Of course, no more introductions to prospective interior decorator clients. That would be disloyal to Marcie, who, dammit, was probably even now inspecting swatches. But suddenly the lunches seemed very important. In fact, they were the only things that had been nice for about a month.

"That little black dress you gave me. Do you remember—the Calvin Klein—the one with the very low back?" She could see Mom registering that the dress was nearly three years old and drawing her own conclusions about how life, and/or Philip and John, had been treating Sandy during the interim period. "You know me," she continued hastily. "I have my favorites. Of all the dresses I've bought since, even when John and I were in Europe, I still love that little dress the best."

Mom beamed with approval. Either Sandy really meant what she said, was flattering—it was always nice to have one's taste endorsed—or she was putting a brave face on her less than perfect circumstances. She was a good girl, it had been fun giving her things, she enjoyed everything so much and wasn't the least bit grasping. Whereas Marcie . . . she sometimes thought that girl had an acquisitive streak.

"I'll walk back to your office with you," she said, "if you don't mind stopping at Saks with me for a moment."

"Oh, I couldn't," Sandy said. "It's really sweet of you but I just couldn't accept it."

"Nonsense, dear. I saw it the other day and I thought to myself, 'that would have looked so pretty with Sandy's black dress. I wonder if she's still got it.' And here you are getting ready to wear it tonight. It's as though it were meant to be."

Sandy looked at the evening bag. It was beautiful. Black, beaded and shiny. And Mom was right, it was as if it had been designed to make her old black dress look like part of a very expensive outfit. But she couldn't take a handout from Mom. She wanted the bag, in fact she was vainly trying to rearrange figures in her head to find a way to buy it for herself. But she didn't want to be given it. Being given a handbag that she couldn't afford to buy for herself now made her feel poorer than not being able to pay the rent. An object of charity, or worse still, pity.

"I just bought a new bag," she said. "I really don't need it. But it was generous of you to think of it."

"Nonsense, dear, a basic black bag is always useful." Turning to the saleslady she said, "That'll be a charge. We'll take it with us."

So Sandy thanked her profusely, for the bag and for lunch, and returned to the office feeling more depressed than she had when she left. She knew that she couldn't call Mom again until her circumstances had improved. And she knew in her heart that once she was on top of the world again she wouldn't bother to call Mom. It didn't make her feel any better about herself.

Nor did her reception at the office. She was, of course, a few minutes late. Well, more like half an hour, actually. But Mom had been a little late and lunch had been leisurely and Saks is hard to get in and out of in under fifteen minutes. Sandy clasped her new purse and the reassuring Saks shopping bag as she stepped back into real life.

"Dammit, Alexis, you're late. The one time you could maybe do something to earn your salary. And where the hell's my cleaning?"

The cleaning was where it had been for the last three days. At the dry cleaner's. Sandy went out for it. It was hot and smoggy; her feet already hurt from walking back from lunch. She hurried, so there wasn't even the distraction of window-shopping, of looking like a smart young matron on her way to some restful, pampering occupation. She looked like what she was: an office girl. But, please God, not for long. In fact, this very afternoon might

172

make all the difference. She was being sent out to show an apartment. Not being sent with enthusiasm—in fact, very reluctantly.
She wished she didn't feel hot and sweaty. That she had time to
prepare herself for her first apartment showing. Cool and confident, showing an apartment to its best advantage. Making sug-
gestions as to how a room could be changed and made to work.

An hour later Sandy was standing outside the apartment
building. She had been there for fifteen minutes. It was hot and
she had a headache. The building was nondescript-modern.
She'd hoped it would have either been so lovely that she and her
prospective client would meet each other's eyes and smile and it
would be all over except the mortgage payments. Or that it would
be hideously run-down and old-fashioned and that she, Sandy,
would point out how by just knocking down a few walls and
adding a window, the three meaningless maids' cells in the rear
would make a studio, or guest room or nursery, depending on
what seemed most appropriate to the client. But neither fantasy
was applicable in this case. So she'd be helpful, friendly, efficient
and full of gentle charm, a quality surely welcome to one who'd
been dealing with real-estate women.

And here came her client. A woman, probably not yet forty,
accompanied by a little dog, was slowly approaching her. Twenty
minutes late and not moving at more than one mile an hour.
Fairly casual, but maybe Sandy was being unfair. It seemed entirely possible that both the woman and her Pekingese were
cruising at their maximum speed. Both small-eyed and overweight, one moving his tiny legs as best he could, the other grind-
ing the thin heels beneath her chubby legs into the pavement.
The Peke carried a lot of fur for a hot day and his tongue hung
out. The woman wore a loose coat buttoned to the neck. An
expensive coat, and above it, time, money and effort had been
spent on hair and face. As always, Sandy wondered, if they cared

173

so much why didn't they just take off weight? Thirty pounds of lard less and who'd need the ounces of lip gloss and grams of hair lacquer?

Sandy had time to consider all this as her client and pet slowly drew to a halt. There was something appalling about the dowagerlike gait of a woman only twelve or thirteen years older than herself. Either the weight or the maintenance to compensate for it, or both, had made this woman stiff, mechanical, Botero-like.

"I'm Alexis Hope," Sandy said, introducing herself in the open, warm, simple way that had done the trick so many times before.

"I'm Mrs. Silvers." She put quite a lot of emphasis on the "Mrs.," as though afraid Sandy might presume some social acquaintance on the basis of this brief encounter. The smile was only the rearrangement of lipstick; the piggy little eyes remained cold. One hand automatically went up to pat her concrete hairdo. Maybe to hear the reassuring jangle of gold jewelry. Once inside, and the coat undone, Sandy saw enough gold to further weigh her down and to allow her walking-around value to fluctuate by several thousand dollars during an active day on the commodities exchange.

As Sandy looked her up and down discretely, she felt herself being less subtly assessed by Mrs. Silvers. Not for a moment did she conceal that she noted the watch as Cartier, but that the shoes and skirt were last year's and, worst of all, no jewelry.

"I was expecting Claudia."

"I'm afraid she's not in the office this afternoon."

"Hm. Let's get on with it, I'm very short of time."

As though Sandy had kept her waiting. Sandy, after explaining herself twice to the doorman who had an imperfect command of English, got the keys and took her client upstairs. They had to wait for the elevator and Mrs. Silvers tapped her little pointed, well-polished toe impatiently.

The apartment was large and completely bare. Bare floors, but not the polished kind. These were the kind that demand wall-to-wall carpeting. Plenty of windows, but modern, metal-surrounded windows. Apart from a conventionally outfitted kitchen, plenty of built-in appliances and similarly designed bathrooms attached to every appropriate room, there was very little to look at. It was a duplex, so Sandy showed the woman eight almost identical, badly proportioned, low-ceilinged rooms. It took less than ten minutes.

"This is the master bedroom . . . and this is another bedroom . . . and this is another . . . er . . . bedroom." There was nothing to add to these bald statements, no little advantages to point out, no enhancing changes to suggest. Then silence, unbroken even when Sandy noticed a small puddle in one corner where the little dog had relieved itself.

Minutes later they were outside the front door, Sandy making a mess of the double lock.

"Well . . ." she said, with an apologetic half-smile.

"Not at all what I wanted. You do know what I want, I hope?"

"Well, actually . . ."

"Next time have them send Claudia. Or if they prefer, I can always try another agency."

The wait for the elevator and the ride down seemed interminable. Sandy was left feeling that, without having done anything wrong, she was going to bear the total blame. The only slightly good thing she could think of was it was Friday afternoon and already the senior employees were sliding off for the weekend. Hence her being allowed to show the apartment. With any luck, her disgrace would not be discovered until after the weekend. That, and the party.

175

For the first time in her life Sandy felt that she was invisible.
Oh, occasionally, not often, she'd started an evening without a
great deal of attention, but it was so easy to be charming and nice
and interested and somebody, usually a man, would be happy to
chat for as long as she wanted.

"I feel invisible," she said, with a smile that qualified the
announcement, and suggested that she was rueful and amused,
not desperate. Made it a reflection on her hostess and fellow
guests, not on herself. Which it damned well was.

"Yais?" Oh God, someone who didn't speak English as his
first language. That made it all immeasurably harder.

"I mean, I don't really know many people here. I feel as
though no one can see me."

He looked at her blankly, but with a slight hint of apprehen-
sion.

"Also me," he said firmly. But kindly, or maybe he was hu-
moring her. "I go get you a dreenk."

"I have one," Sandy said, indicating an almost full glass of
white wine in her hand.

"I be right back," he said, and moved away. She never saw him
again. Fairly insulting, but also mysterious. There were only
fourteen places set for dinner, and she still hadn't spotted him by
the time they sat down.

"If he'd left the house, we'd be an uneven number—thirteen—
it'd be a catastrophe. And surely I couldn't have scared him that
much. Do you think he's put on a disguise?"

Her left-hand neighbor laughed, patted her hand.

"You're a funny gal," he said. Sandy was so grateful for a
moment's appreciation that she almost forgot how jarring the
word "gal" always seemed to her.

He left his hand on hers for a moment, almost absentmindedly,
as he responded to a remark about a football game from a man

across the table. Sandy looked at him. Just as handsome as his photographs. Pity she hadn't seen any of his recent movies. John hadn't been a great moviegoer, and now she lacked the money or energy to go on her own. He was very tanned, tall and broad, and his shirt had reassuringly hard bulges where the muscles strained the material. Sandy wasn't looking for the outward symbols of virility. She was looking for a man who looked as though he could take care of himself and her too. Better still, he was, though she didn't put it that way, the dominant male in this group. Which meant that the woman under his protection got little extra perks like deference and respect. He was very Western in a Ralph Lauren way. Sandy really preferred men in well-cut, pin-stripe suits with fat silk ties and substantial cuff links, but they didn't grow on huckleberry bushes. She might have been happier with someone who didn't carry quite so much of that blue-green sort of Indian stone on his person, but . . . well, try to be adaptable.

"Alexis . . ."—a female voice from across the table. Sandy looked up, returned Denise's bright smile. But with reservation. Apart from her host and hostess, Denise was the only person at the party who Sandy knew. In fact, the only other single girl. So Sandy'd made straight for her, not exactly presuming an acquaintanceship, but doing the only thing possible in the circumstances—the circumstances being a hostess who meticulously introduced each arrival to all the other guests, but by name only. So in effect, it was like an assembly line introduction ending with abandonment. It never occurred to her to introduce an actual person, not just a name. In her desperation, Sandy would have settled for: "Sandy, I'd like you to meet Oswald, he's interested in church architecture." As it was, she'd greeted Denise enthusiastically, and had been firmly snubbed. Probably nothing personal, just that she had a new man and didn't want there to be any possibility of her losing him to the only other unattached girl in the room.

177

"I saw a friend of yours at lunch."

"Oh?"

"At 21."

Sandy wasn't sure which way this conversation was going, but from Denise's air of tantalization and self-congratulation she deduced it wasn't going to be good. So she said nothing.

"John."

"John who?" Sandy's heart began to pound, but she managed to keep her voice expressionless.

Denise was not to be so easily deflected. She laughed, a high tinkling attention-getting laugh. And got some attention. Stuart, on Sandy's left, turned away from discussing the deficiencies of referees, both in terms of morality and eyesight, and was listening.

"Don't you want to know who he was with?" Encouraged by a larger audience, she was now openly teasing.

"Not particularly." Sandy's voice was low but steady, as she started to feel tears of humiliation welling in her eyes.

"I don't blame you—very tacky, silicone tits and bleached hair."

Sandy said nothing. She couldn't. Her life seemed to her almost unbearable, even without thinking of John. She missed him desperately, benefits apart. But she'd assumed that he'd gone back to his wife. Although she hadn't dwelt on it while he was around, she knew he'd run out of money. And that was why he'd left her. But to be in the same city, lunching out, with someone else. Now she really felt abandoned, humiliated.

"Now, don't be upset. She's nothing like as attractive as you are. She's the girl from that jeans commercial, you know . . ." And she began to hum a familiar and irritating jingle.

Sandy knew she couldn't bear to hear the actual name. At the same time she remembered an old boyfriend, in England, when she'd been about eighteen—she hadn't thought of him in years—and something he'd said. He'd been describing some boat voyage, from Barcelona to Majorca, or something, and explaining how he'd avoided being seasick. "It was beastly rough, and they were throwing up all over the place. The boat stunk of olive oil and garlic even before. I felt like nothing on earth, but then I said to myself, "Look here, you're English. Can't disgorge on the deck, let the side down. So I didn't." At the time, Sandy, though never overjudgmental as far as men were concerned, had been mildly amused; later she'd been scornful. Now she was coming around to his way of thinking. Impossible to make an exhibition of herself in front of these . . . these foreigners.

"Really, Denise, you're wonderful. Do you know the words to lots of television commercials? But we shouldn't chat about people who the others haven't met. It's boring for them and rude to our hostess."

"So you've had a rough time?"

The first actual bit of face-to-face conversation they'd had all evening. Though, to be literal, his face was pointing straight ahead, his fists clenched and his foot ineffectually braking on the carpeted floor of the vintage Bentley. His driver was livening up what had evidently been a long and boring evening by challenging taxis and red lights. Or maybe he'd had a drink or two. Sandy was young enough to believe death was for other people. Besides, if she had to die young, let it be in a chauffeur-driven car, accompanied by a movie star, on the way back from a fashionable Manhattan party. Headlines and so forth.

"Not really, just a love affair that broke up. All over now." No need to sound either pathetic or pining over an absent lover. No point in sounding like a loser. No point in putting him off. Not exactly her type, but quite nice. Maybe he'd call her. Preferably at the office, just the thing to make the girls sit up and take notice. Or, better still, maybe he'd come and collect her. For lunch. No argument about who got stuck with the phones that day.

But for that to happen, some form of human communication should take place. After dinner she'd sat next to him, but was not exactly part of the conversation. He'd mainly addressed himself to two middle-aged men. They'd lighted her cigarettes and filled her glass. Stuart had patted her leg and squeezed her thigh in a nonlascivious way from time to time. Occasionally, they would include her. From one, an "Isn't that so, little lady?" And from the other, a smile which was meant to reassure her, to make sure she understood the rough talk was all in jest. The first time she'd made some kind of effort to join in she was greeted with a remark about how cute her accent was and how one of them had always had English secretaries. And the second time with a polite, if slightly startled, smile followed by a swift return to the subject, her input ignored. Not that she much minded. She was tired, and the food and wine, both of a now unaccustomed quality, had left her sleepy. The cigarettes, from her hostess's Baccarat box on the coffee table—she didn't normally smoke, at least hadn't since John had left her and she'd had to buy and carry her own—made her slightly dizzy. But she felt no wish to go home early. Denise might be hostile, she might have been ignored by the other guests, her hosts might have been less than totally thoughtful (tonight) or gracious (in the past), but all that was swept aside. She was undoubtedly "with" the most visible man in the room. Not the richest, nor the most powerful, since only the most tragically naive hostess would invite an actor to play either of those roles. But she was certainly sitting by, had been claimed by, the man for whom the party had been given. The guest of honor. It was both exhilarating in the sense of being new and exciting, and at the same time immensely reassuring in its familiarity.

Sandy liked to be around movie people. She had no actual

ambitions herself, but since it was unlikely she'd spend the rest of her life in America she wanted some respectable reason for having been there. Better to be able to say, in London, ". . . divine little house in Palm Springs. My husband was involved in the movie industry then . . . ," than to claim that she was married to someone who'd made a bundle selling life insurance in the greater Los Angeles area.

"It's very kind of you to drive me home," she said, for want of a more inspired conversation starter. "I love your car."

That did it. She got a very full rundown on the relative virtues of every car ever made, ending with the inevitable conclusion that this particular model, while not as expensive as some, was by far the best performer, the most beautiful and preferable to all others.

At least one of them was talking. Sandy knew many men preferred a good listener to a good talker. Which was fine, but how was he going to get to know her? She had to make some impression during the next three or four minutes or she would be just one more pretty face.

"Um," she interrupted tentatively, "you go right on Park and then . . ."

"Can you ask me up for a drink?"

"No, I . . . er . . ." she scrambled around for a suitable excuse. Her apartment was in no way helpful to the kind of image she was trying to project.

"Okay, we'll have a drink at my hotel." He didn't seem interested in an explanation. Sandy would have been more pleased by being invited, rather than press-ganged, but even so she was going to have a chance to get to know him better.

"Oh, lovely. But I really shouldn't be too late. I've got a lot to do in the morning."

"Sure."

The car deposited them. Keys and messages were picked up at

the reception desk. Sandy felt a slight pang of anxiety. The reception clerk was one who had handed her keys day after day when she'd been staying at this hotel with John. She'd always been aloof, compensating for the fact that she wasn't yet married to John, to stress that she soon would be and should be treated as a wife, not a mistress. She took a deep breath, drew herself up straight, and looked him in the eye. He met her gaze without a flicker of recognition. So either he was super tactful, which was in a strange way pretty insulting, or he really didn't recognize her. That wasn't exactly ideal either.

Stuart started away from the desk, then turned back.

"Look, there's this girl. Black, name of Francine. She's been bothering me. If she comes, tell her I checked out. Okay?"

The reception clerk nodded, without a hint of curiosity. Sandy, while acknowledging that it was hard on Stuart to be hounded by fans and crazy people, felt for a moment sorry for Francine, whoever she might be. For one second she had an image of John saying to the same receptionist: "There's this girl, English, called Alexis . . ." But that was different.

The suite, fortunately, was not the one in which she'd stayed with John. But the bowls of complimentary fruit and the wilting rose in a small vase, left over from a room service tray, brought back memories of a series of hotel rooms. Home for Sandy and John. These red roses she'd ignored, while at the Carlyle she'd kept the tiny vases of sweetheart roses and dotted them about the suite. And what was the name of that hotel in Paris? Maybe L'Hôtel, with a single dark blue iris on the side of the tub. And the tuberoses—that time when she'd bought an armful and filled the entire bedroom with that sweet, erotic smell. Associations, flowers and luxury, scents and sex. All the above and John. Sandy was well aware that all the things that made her nostalgic for John cost money. But that didn't mean she was greedy; it was just there'd been no shared moment of pleasure which hadn't involved the expenditure of money or the exclusion of the masses. A winter walk on a deserted public beach wasn't John's style. His own cabana at the better end of the best swimming pool was. Passionate lovemaking could not take place in the back of a car or in the grass, it had to be between those ridiculous Porthault sheets she'd once craved, in a room set to blood temperature in winter and almost at freezing point in the middle of summer. And she was aware that there was something of that in her too. Something that needed to be shown that she was worth a little more. In a fairy tale it might have been a dragon slain; in real life it tended to be tax deductible sacrifices. Largely symbolic, since she had very little to show for it.

Stuart poured them both glasses of champagne. She took one, sipped. The last thing she wanted was another drink. But his gesture seemed appropriate, reassuring.

At a loss for something to say or do, Sandy crossed to the window. In someone's home, she might have looked over a bookshelf, or admired a painting. In a hotel suite there isn't much in the way of what Mom used to call "conversation pieces." So Sandy looked out the window at the familiar and uninspiring view. Stuart followed her and almost immediately she felt a firm masculine arm around her waist, drawing her to him. Sandy felt her eyes close, her body relax. It was like being very sleepy and tumbling into a large soft bed. After a moment she pulled back, trying to find that thin line between being ridiculously prudish and getting into something she couldn't handle. She desperately groped around for something light and sophisticated to say. Something that would hint to him that she *might* be available. In time. And that she would be well worth having, but that it would involve a commitment. That she was neither cold nor loose. That she was sophisticated enough to accept his embrace and kiss as a tribute to her beauty and not to assume it was a premature pass.

The telephone rang before she could find a way of expressing all this. And Stuart, who was trying to get her back into his arms, left her to go and answer it.

"Yes. Who? I don't know anyone of that name." A pause. His hand not quite covering the mouthpiece, he said to Sandy, "Goddamn switchboard operators." Then, back into the mouthpiece, "Well, tell her there's no reply. And hold all other calls till I tell you."

He put the phone down, picked up the champagne bottle and waved an arm toward the sofa. "Sit down."

Sandy sat. "No more for me, thank you." He filled her glass, ignoring her.

Then he put the bottle on the table and turned toward her. She raised the glass to her lips, to ward off another attack, more than to take a drink. When she lowered it, he took it with one hand, putting it on the table. The other he put firmly around her shoulders, and drew her down to him. The warmth of his body made Sandy feel safe, but she wished he'd say something from time to time. She lay there, poised to jump away when he came on too strong, but feeling that a strong stand for her virtue was at the moment premature. After all, he hadn't done anything. But that was part of the trouble. He hadn't tried to put a hand up her shirt, but neither had he made any effort to get to know her on any other level. She realized he probably didn't know her second name. She had the impression that he was confused about her in some way. Didn't know how to deal with her. Which was how she felt about him. Other men—John and Philip, for instance— had, during the courtship stages at least, drawn her out. They'd amused her, given her cues to be amusing back. Maybe that'd been a mixed blessing. It sure hadn't been an accurate picture of things to come.

A moment later she revised the hand up her skirt bit. Nor was the attack, when it came, very subtle. A large strong hand slid firmly under her dress and gripped a breast. Trying to avoid the appearance of a struggle, Sandy took the hand gently and removed it.

"What's wrong. Don't you like me?"

"Of course I like you. Very much. But we hardly know each other."

Stuart looked puzzled, rather in the manner of one who can't remember whether he turned the gas off before leaving home on a world cruise. Sandy imagined they were on the verge of a breakthrough. But Stuart got up and put on some music. Nothing very original. A best-of-Sinatra medley.

Sandy sat up, tried to push her hair into place. She was glancing around for a mirror when Stuart returned. He slid her down on the sofa and lay beside her, half on top. Sandy hesitated. No time for delicate hints here. Time to go home.

"Please. No. Please let me up."

Stuart hesitated a second, then slipped a shoulder strap down Sandy's arm and whispered into her neck.

"Everything's all right. I love you."

Sandy woke up slowly. She didn't open her eyes immediately. She had a headache and her eyes felt crusty and gummy. Her first thought was that she must have gone to bed with her make-up on. Not something she usually did. The second was that not only did her head hurt but her mouth was dry. So were her lips.

She didn't know where she was. The room was light, she could tell that much. She decided to keep her eyes shut until she was awake enough to remember. The bed felt comfortable and large. The room was air-conditioned. There was something permanent and good about it. If only she felt better. A hangover and lack of sleep. If she just dropped off for another ten minutes she'd wake up fine. But what time was it? She mustn't be late for work. No, it was Saturday and . . . It all came back at once. It was Saturday and everything was all right. Or it would be if she had just a little more sleep. She turned her head slightly and opened one eye. Checking if Stuart was still asleep. She hoped so. If she felt like hell, she probably looked like it too. There was no one there. She closed her eyes, as though playing for time, then gingerly put her right arm out and patted his side of the bed. No one there. It would be lovely to go back to sleep, but Sandy was in the business of pleasing people. And one of the fastest ways to start a day not pleasing someone was to give him a quick blast of early morning breath. Followed up by greeting him with sleep smudged eyes with yucky bits of mascara goo in the corners. She sat up like a little trooper and immediately felt slightly sick. Quick glance around, then a dash for the bathroom. Once the door was firmly locked behind her she turned on the lights, one by one, adjusting the rheostat until she had full theatrical lighting. The result was even grimmer than she'd feared. However, life must go on and Sandy went to work. In her own bathroom there were all the necessary materials, but here a little ingenuity was necessary. First to try to feel slightly better. A quick pee, a glass of water, couple of Bufferins, then clean the teeth. Um, just one toothbrush. No time for squeamishness now. She brushed her teeth thoroughly and carefully put the top back on the toothpaste and dried and replaced the toothbrush exactly where she'd found it. No point in drawing attention to having borrowed it. Both John and Philip had taught her that men could be really picky about small bathroom things. Philip had once lost his temper when she'd borrowed his razor and John, who had once been more than happy to put any part of her in his mouth while in bed, would behave as though violated if she touched any implement he might be eating with, let alone his sacred toothbrush. And though Stuart was more, well, out-of-doorsy than either of his predecessors, there was no point in taking chances. Especially

186

since Sandy was planning to generally tidy up and civilize him.

She wrapped her hair in a towel, cleaned her face as best she could with some suntan lotion she found in the medicine chest, and stepped into the bath. She felt a little better already, soaking the stiffness out of her tired and fairly sore body. That was another area where she'd have to teach Stuart something. Her role was that of a delicate flower, gently tended and admired, and made love to. Not to be jumped on quite as violently as last night. As far as she could remember, Stuart had made his name in a series of rodeo movies. It showed.

Her purse was in the living room, so there was no possibility of making up, but she borrowed his comb, applied a warm damp facecloth to the remains of the suntan lotion, wrapped a large white towel seductively around herself, and went into the living room. Ready to find Stuart, order a little light breakfast to eat in bed, get up gradually and go out somewhere really nice for lunch. Preferably somewhere that served a really good Bloody Mary.

"Hello, English." Stuart was seated at a room-service table, reading the trades. "Coffee?"

"Good morning," Sandy said, with a halfhearted Dietrich imitation, intended to elicit some comment on her garb. But Stuart was already back into his paper. Not much of a talker at breakfast. But that wasn't entirely surprising. He wasn't much of a talker, at any rate to women, at dinner either. She'd never quite gotten his attention until they were on the sofa. But he loved her, he'd said it and he'd showed it in bed. It might all take time, but it'd be all right.

She poured herself some coffee, trying not to see the remains of a rare steak.

"Want something to eat?"

"Perhaps a croissant."

"There're some muffins under that dish."

Sandy took half a muffin. Not quite the same thing. But it made her feel better. So did a selection of the complimentary fruit.

Stuart remained silent, except for some rather noisy slurping of coffee. Sandy finished her breakfast. Nothing happened. After a moment she got up and went and got dressed. Her dress was crushed and she hated putting on last night's pantyhose. Then, rather at a loss, she returned to the breakfast table. She was thrown by being right back where she came in, as it were. Surely the intimacies of last night should have advanced the relationship somewhat.

"You're off?" He didn't rise from his seat, and continued to drink his coffee. Sandy felt a wave of panic rise from her stomach. For a moment she thought she might be going to throw up. "Come back tonight at eight, okay?" Not the most gracious invitation she'd ever received, but the feeling of relief was almost overwhelming. She went over to him and kissed him, put her arms around him and squeezed him. Not so cool, she knew that she was appearing almost grateful. But he seemed pleased, if surprised, and looked at her with an expression of kindness which prompted her to blurt out:

"And I love you, too."

"Sure, kid. You're cute. Run along now. I've got business to attend to." And he gave her a little slap on the bottom. Sandy was genuinely interested to hear what kind of business he attended to on Saturday mornings, but the pat on the ass was clearly dismissive.

So Sandy left. She wasn't sure how to get home. She didn't have a car and hoped she had enough money for a taxi. Her evening coat was conservative, fortunately, but even so she felt conspicuous descending in the elevator and crossing the lobby with it buttoned up tightly, wearing evening shoes and carrying

Mom's super-dressy evening bag. The hotel staff had seen it all before—so often she didn't merit a second glance. But a couple of tourists from out of town who expected exotic goings-on in this famous hotel had their morning made. They stared, unabashed, then discussed her, whispering behind raised hands, their eyes never leaving her.

The doorman, who'd often hailed John's car for her, and had even, on occasion, called her "Madam," gave her no more than a disdainful glance before stepping out to hail a cab. She decided to take a cab. If she didn't have enough money to get the whole way home at least she could go part of the way. It took him several minutes to get one, and every one of them was humiliating. Sandy had never imagined so many people crossed the portals of the hotel at ten o'clock in the morning. Seemingly hundreds of familiar employees streamed around. A couple of tired businessmen looked her up and down, accurately assessing how she'd spent the night.

Sandy held her head high, vainly trying to think of an alternative explanation for her appearance. A sort of alibi, however improbable. An exercise in method acting.

As she waited for the taxi, she started to make a mental list of what she'd put in her overnight bag that evening. In a way, though hardly chivalrous, Stuart had done her a favor by telling her to come over to his suite, instead of collecting her. This way she could dump a nightdress, cosmetics and something suitable for Sunday mornings in the bedroom before they went out. Maybe it was his way of being tactful, making it easy for her. She might have been underestimating him. Last night, he'd seemed almost boorish and it had turned out that he didn't know how to bring himself to tell her he loved her. Tomorrow, when she left the hotel, she'd wear something perhaps a little dressier than she'd originally planned. She'd be perfectly groomed, look like one of the better guests. The next day she'd bring an outfit or two. So she could go directly to the office. Though, God willing, she would probably give notice in a day or two. The trick was to act with dignity now and act the same way tomorrow, and when they started to accept her as a resident in the hotel they'd remember nothing odd about this morning. She wondered if Stuart was, had ever been, married. It was, perhaps, a little early to think about that. But she had been in the habit of being swept off her feet. Dennis, Philip, John. She'd known none of them for longer than this without something concrete being understood. Love at first sight. No wonder she believed in it. And now Stuart. It was like a feeling of spring. She stepped lightly into the cab, and gave the address of her apartment.

Once home, she looked at the unattractive apartment with new eyes. They'd been through some hard times together; now it was time for the parting of the ways. First the hotel, and then she'd start looking around for a house. She had a pleasurable five minutes trying to decide whether to use the agency she worked for and really making them sweat, or whether it would be more fun to use their closest rival.

By now it was ten-thirty, and some decisions had to be made about how to spend the day. Sandy would have liked to call Diane and tell her that her luck had changed. But Saturday mornings Philip didn't work and he was quite likely to answer the telephone. So that was out. It would be fun to go and buy some new clothes, in anticipation of her new financial status, but there were practical difficulties: no money in her checking account, no valid credit cards. Time enough for all that, and it might be tactful and fun to have Stuart come along on that first shopping trip. Make him buy himself some more conservative clothes. It could be done if she flattered him. Gradually make him over.

But in the meantime, maintenance. She took off her dress and hung it carefully in the bathroom, to allow the steam to take the creases out. She took off her pantyhose and underwear and soaked them in Woolite. She'd need the pantyhose tonight; they were her only pair without a run. She went to her wardrobe, chose her second-best outfit, since Stuart had already seen her best. Pity he hadn't given her some clue about what they were going to do that evening. Since he was so casually dressed she wouldn't end up being underdressed, but it was necessary to be glamorous. She finally chose a white silk shirt and an elegant black straight skirt. Fortunately both were timeless, since they dated back to early Philip days. Exactly how timeless they were she'd checked a few weeks past. She'd gone into the same store and tried on this year's plain silk shirt and plain black skirt. Two-thirds of an inch on the hemline, fortunately shorter, so she'd simply taken the skirt up with no telltale lines. A few minor changes in seams, but no one would be able to tell the difference. She checked both garments carefully for stains or creases, then checked and polished her shoes and handbag. Eleven-fifteen. She recleaned her face, fed it all kinds of moisturizing and rejuvenating unguents. Most of the jars were nearly empty. Something that had been worrying her, since she knew that when it came to replacing them, she would have to go to the corner drugstore and buy a nice sensible jar of good old Ponds' instead of dropping in at Janet Sartin and picking up whatever was required. She looked at her pandalike face—a thin white mask with small greasy areas around the eyes and mouth—with satisfaction. That should do the trick.

Then an aspirin and a Valium. She closed the curtains, set her alarm for four in order to give herself plenty of time to wash her hair and touch up her manicure, and got into bed. For a moment, she considered taking the telephone off the hook, then decided not to. It was Saturday, not a day when a bank or landlord was likely to call. And if Mom or Diane called to chat, so much the better. She wanted to share her good news with someone.

191

Sandy sighed. That was not like her. She rarely complained about anything, and when she did it was in a polite, straightforward way. Sighing, nagging and whining, along with gaining weight, not washing one's hair, and having chipped nail polish had to be permanently forsaken by anyone who wanted to excel in the business of pleasing people. Not that Sandy, in a million years, would have thought of herself like that. She was in—or on the fringes of—the real-estate business. She was nice to people, tried to be a good person, and people treated her well. Which made the behavior of the people in the real-estate office all the more confusing and hurtful. And naturally men fell in love with her and wanted to do things for her. But she did things for them too.

So when she sighed it was like another—a lesser—woman screaming. And she expected to have the same results. But Stuart said nothing, not even giving her the little absentminded pat on the knee which she already understood to be both reassuring and dismissive.

"I'm hungry." She was, but what she really meant was she was bored. Not an ideal evening. It had started well. She'd looked wonderful, and Stuart had been pleased to see her. Drinks had been poured, then drunk. Conversation had been a little slow, but Sandy had decided not to take it personally. She'd been relieved almost as much as excited when he sat down beside her and kissed her. He'd started to undo the buttons on her blouse and she'd taken it and her skirt off to preserve them for later in the evening. She didn't want to look a mess at dinner.

This time Sandy was more receptive and confident than she'd been the night before. Afterward, Stuart had rolled over with a groan and Sandy had gone into the bathroom to do twenty minutes of repair work on her face and hair. When she'd come out, he'd been sitting up in bed watching television. She'd lain down on the bed beside him. That'd been two hours ago.

"I'm hungry," she said again.

"This show'll be over in half an hour."

"But it's ten-thirty. Most places will be closed. Do you want me to call and make a reservation?"

"Why don't you call room service?"

Room service. Room service for breakfast or a late-night, post-lovemaking snack was romantic. Room service for a date definitely didn't make it. Room service was not what this carefully preserved silk shirt was for. It wasn't what three hours of hairdressing and making up and rejecting the first version was for. It wasn't what diet and exercise were for.

"Room service?"

"Yeah. Order what you like. Get me a steak and salad and some chocolate ice cream."

She didn't have much choice. She could either do as he said or go home. She had a feeling it didn't make much difference to him at the moment. Later, of course, he'd miss her. But he seemed to be so wrapped up in this idiotic television show. Not even a movie or a special, just a regular television series. Probably he had some professional interest in it. If he'd told her what it was exactly she'd have been happy to watch with him. But it was the second or maybe even third program he'd watched. Respecting Philip's special privileges as a writer was one thing. Tedious but understandable, since that was how he'd supported her. But to tiptoe around someone watching an American version of a spaghetti Western was absurd.

"All right," she said, trying to inject a little good-sport intonation into her voice, "but tomorrow we go somewhere nice for lunch. Deal?"

"Sure, kid, whatever you say."

And another thing—but she would have to deal with this one at a later date—he'd have to stop calling her "English" and "kid" and so forth. So what would he call her? Time for Sandy again, it would go better with the fresh-air image she would now probably be going for.

Sandy ordered dinner. There didn't seem to be anything on the menu that she was hungry for. What she really wanted was candlelight and an attentive waiter and people looking at her and Stuart with admiration and curiosity. And, almost as an after-thought, a few tiny slices of thinly cut veal and a small green salad. Instead she was going to get a rather solid omelette. The club sandwich was almost tempting, but Sandy had trained herself not to eat bread, let alone mayonnaise. She got dressed again to let the waiter in, which left her forty-five minutes to kill. She perched on the end of the bed to watch the television, but was unable to concentrate on the complicated but nevertheless familiar plot. She got up and wandered into the other room. As she did so Stuart shot her a glance which seemed almost irritated. She sat in an armchair and leafed through a hotel room pseudo magazine. Several amazingly boring travel articles and lots of advertisements. Advertisements, as in *Vogue*, could keep Sandy as happy as Conrad might a seafaring man. But the advertisements were for a category of goods which Sandy not only couldn't afford but didn't want. Wildly expensive, amazingly ugly jewelry. Another more curious person, Diane for instance, might have spent a happy moment or two trying to imagine the woman who would want to spend forty-seven thousand dollars plus tax on a sapphire, ruby and diamond pin depicting Donald Duck. Flick. Over to a large color photograph of a maroon Cadillac. She wanted a maroon Cadillac about as much as she wanted a mink stole. And so on. That filled about three minutes. A scathing glance at the seemingly acrylic Gauguin reproduction on the wall took up nearly twenty seconds. Sandy fought an impulse to drum her fingers on the coffee table. Death to a manicure. She did a couple of isometric tummy flattening exercises and sighed again.

Her attempts to mildly glamorize dinner were swiftly foiled by Stuart. She was just getting the table set up in the living room, a chair on either side, the lights dimmed, music on and in the midst of negotiations with the waiter for candles—a commodity which he denied having ever heard of—when Stuart, dressed attractively but hardly conventionally with a towel wrapped around his waist, looked into the living room.

"Whaddya doing?"

"Dinner is served," Sandy said.

"There's no TV in that room. Bring it in here."

Soon they were seated in the bedroom, Stuart perched on the end of the bed, Sandy seated on a chair, but at a three-quarters angle to the television so that Stuart constantly seemed to be looking over her shoulder like a trapped guest at a cocktail party. The distracting noise without vision continued. If Sandy hadn't been so confused she'd have been angry. As it was she felt jumpy, unsure.

"That all you're having? I thought you were hungry."

"I am." She was slightly defensive. "But I have to watch my figure."

That was the kind of remark, when made by other women, that made Sandy wince. Better get a grip on herself.

"Oh?" he said, not interested. At least, having been coy, she expected some response in the hackneyed order of "No, you don't," or even "I'll watch it for you." Something.

Not much more was said during dinner, the whole meal taking about twelve minutes. Sandy wondered if she might be going to cry. She made one last effort, and when there was a commercial break, asked, "What'll we do tomorrow? Let's make a plan. Something, you know, different. Let's go to the Village . . . or . . . I don't know, an art exhibition or go riding in the park."

Stuart was looking at her as though she were insane but not actually dangerous. In truth, she did sound a little potty to herself.

"Look, kid, I've got to go out of town for a couple of days. Thought I'd told you."

"Oh?"

"Got to get an early start tomorrow."

"But tomorrow's Sunday."

"Yeah. Real early. Got to get a good night's sleep."

"Maybe I should go home," Sandy heard herself say, but she didn't know whether she'd said it as a veiled threat or a cry for reassurance. Or maybe it was just her pride suggesting it before he did.

Stuart's face cleared. He looked relieved.

"Yeah, maybe. I'm really bushed."

"When'll you be back?"

"Day or two, I don't know yet."

A short silence.

"You don't have my telephone number."

"Give it to me."

Sandy got up and wrote her number on the bedside pad.

"And I don't have yours." She tried to imply that though it would be mere politeness for him to give her the number, she would, of course, never use it. That she was not in the habit of telephoning men. She might not have been completely successful because he said:

"I'm always at this hotel when I'm here."

"Oh. Well. Of course."

It really was rather rude. Sandy made a mental note that next time he wasn't going to get her to bed before dinner. Then she'd have a little more control over the situation.

196

She went to the closet and got her coat. It would have been nice if he'd gotten up to fetch it for her. She hoped that when she left he wouldn't just be sitting at the table, chewing slowly and watching television. Instead he was sealing an envelope. She crossed the room quickly, not wanting to seem to be hanging around.

"Bye, bye. Sleep well. I love you." She put her arms around him and gave him a kiss. Again not drawing it out.

"Me, too. I'll call you."

They went to the door. He opened it. Again there was a moment's hesitation between them.

"Well, good-bye."

But she couldn't leave that second. He'd taken her purse, opened it and popped in an envelope. So he'd changed his mind about his telephone number. And knowing how inarticulate he was, maybe he'd written something he couldn't say. In the elevator, she opened the envelope. Fortunately, she was alone, so there was no one to see her face when she found two neatly folded hundred-dollar bills.

Chapter Ten

"Someone—not me, God knows—but someone at some time must have suggested you get what remains of your head shrunk."

"Yes, it has come up from time to time."

Claire picked a piece of fried chicken out of the box. Diane looked with mild disgust and followed the suggestion she should put something in her mouth by lighting another cigarette.

"But you assume it wouldn't be worth it, it would take years and by then you'd have smoked yourself to death. And probably those around you, too."

"I should have bought stock in the Colonel the day I moved out. Don't you ever cook anything?"

"Sure, look in the freezer. Succulent baby crayfish, caught at dawn and marinated in sake, with steamed savage rice and . . ."

"Savage rice?"

"That's what they call the rice with all those pieces of black in it on Air France."

"Cooking, in my opinion, doesn't just mean nicking stuff off the airlines."

"Well, I usually dress it up with a little ketchup."

"Before I was just not hungry. Now I'm definitely sick."

"So?"

"So what?"

"So what're you going to do about cleaning up your act?"

"I don't know."

"So like I said, maybe Freud could help, since even I have failed. But I'm probably being too modest."

"It's your worst fault."

"And?" Claire asked. And after no reply, added: "Dammit, just for once, maybe the first time, I'm not joking. You can't go on like this. You've got to find a way to give it up."

"And then what would I have?"

A matched pair. Diane and Linda. Linda and Diane. They were making David uneasy. He was not indifferent to the pleasures of their parallel tongues tracing a line slowly down either side of his cock. Nor to one pair of lips, when they arrived simultaneously at the tip, gently nudging away the other and, with no change of pace, taking him inside her mouth and moving back toward the roots, swallowing him, pausing and then, at the same speed, retracing her path. Releasing him for the other eager, waiting mouth.

But this wasn't the same deal as, for instance, the time he'd picked up those two kids, hitchhiking back from the beach. Healthy summer children, far too young to have seen *Blow Up* and far too mindless to understand that, while not exactly destroying themselves, they were throwing away or wasting some essential innocence or beauty. And there'd been a certain pleasurable risk involved. They happily, willingly, lived up to his fantasies, and he was aware he might be called upon to live up to theirs. He couldn't count on either girl to fake it if he failed to deliver. The symmetry of their actions excited him, but they'd moved as a team and this made him anxious. They seemed capable of, likely to, gang up on him.

Not so Diane. He'd done this before with Linda, without it being very important to either of them. But the intensity of Diane's feelings were stifling him. He knew they were on a course of such destruction that he feared her. She'd made it clear that she loved him and now there was an unspoken agreement that he couldn't leave her as long as she was totally subservient. It was as if he were presenting her with a series of tests. Until she failed one he would never be free of her. Each time he would somehow ask her to go further and, however pain-filled her silence might be, she refused him nothing. There were even times when he thought she might end up the winner. The whole deal scared him, he didn't understand how it had evolved, but he knew theirs was a situation from which hideous inexplicable things came. He'd wondered once if she would kill for him. He'd also wondered if he mightn't be capable of asking her to.

And though she willingly gave whatever he asked, there was still an element of her that eluded him. As though he'd broken her but was unable to degrade her. There was some quality in her, so lacking in him, that saved her. That was probably what he wanted to destroy. Would have to destroy if he was ever to be completely rid of her.

Like now. There was nothing he could demand that they, each for different reasons, wouldn't perform. But they reserved gentleness, respect even, it seemed to him for one another. When he demanded they make love to one another, for him to watch, although neither would have any wish to do so were he not there, he was made to feel they gave to each other something neither had ever given him. When he made love to Linda afterward, deliberately choosing her over Diane, he was taken aback to find, on coming and raising his head, Diane and Linda tightly holding one another's hands, and Diane stroking Linda's hair. As though comforting a child.

Diane's aunt, who had a strange habit of cheerfully repeating the most unkind observations and gossip without ever suggesting she'd offered even token defense or denial, once told Diane that the vicar's wife had said she, Diane, would end in the gutter. Diane replied disrespectfully but was in a way not unpleased. They had just gotten to Verlaine and Baudelaire in senior French, and she was already drawn to Rimbaud. Anyway, ending up in the gutter seemed infinitely preferable to ending up like the vicar's wife: facial hair, yellow teeth and a terror to a seemingly endless stream of adenoidal and underpaid servant girls.

Since then her views on life had changed. She'd laughed when she'd seen a line of sexy underwear in France called Fleurs du Mal, and Baudelaire had lost some of his earlier appeal. But killing yourself should qualify you for the gutter remark, she supposed. And killing herself seemed the most logical thing to do. Also the most sensible, the neatest course of action.

Not that she'd do it, of course. She wasn't, as people had in the past rather patronizingly told her, the suicidal type. But she was unable to come up with a more attractive second choice. For the first time she missed Jan's awful squalid apartment. If she still lived there she could lock herself in, get drunk, sleep twelve hours and then reassess her position. But she didn't. The drunk part seemed practical, though. She'd go to the nearest bar, have a couple of large drinks and try to think clearly.

The decision to get drunk was not one which usually caused self-congratulation in Diane. But at least it was action of a sort. Better than standing here in the middle of the sidewalk in the blazing sun.

She started to walk along the street and realized she was only half a dozen blocks from the Plaza. Much better. It would be quiet and dark and cool. There would be less fear of interruption there than in a bar. And she had time to spare. She was in no hurry to go home. In no hurry to resume her life in any way at all. If she couldn't face the idea of an evening with Philip, how was she going to manage the rest of her life. She felt beaten by his dislike, his reserve, his unhappiness. And more immediately, more dramatically beaten by David. He had won. After this afternoon she mustn't, couldn't see him again. And to go on living, having discarded her obsession, seemed impossible. And she knew in her heart she couldn't make it. She might hold out for a week, then one day, junkielike, she'd pick up the phone and call him. And he, unenthusiastically, would make a date. God knows what he'd have lined up for next time. It wasn't possible.

But she was an adult, educated, living in a free country, able to speak the language. It was ridiculous to think like this. She could change her life. She had before. The old running-away game. Only she couldn't think of anywhere to run to anymore. What would one of her fictional heroines do now? The main trouble with fictional heroines was that they were usually very pretty. You could be quite sure that Iris Storm only became paler and more elegantly thin as syphilis took its grip. Holly Golightly would end up with a TV dinner if she'd suffered from acne. Jane Eyre would have moved from family to family, ending up in a boarding house living on her modest savings. Camille in a charity ward. Tess would have stayed on the farm.

She knew in her heart what she was supposed to do. What pride and honor demanded. She should leave Philip. Move back with Claire or get a small apartment. There wasn't even the excuse of Tania. Philip's relief would be so great that he'd let her have Tania, and even subsidize her to a modest extent. She didn't for a moment imagine that his sense of relief at her departure would set in motion any wild generosity. But it could be done. It could be done if she could deal with day-care centers, a nine-to-five job, staying in at night except for when she could afford a baby-sitter, doing her own laundry and housework. And ironing. Suddenly the image of Jan's apartment seemed horrible. If she'd been so unable to cope with that life by herself, how would she manage with a child. And not taking Tania was unthinkable.

What has happened to me, she thought. She'd run out of energy, of courage. Depression was paralyzing her. I've become Sandy—except here again, like the fictional heroines, Sandy had the redeeming graces of charm and beauty and gaiety. Coming to America had been a kind of gamble. At home there were limited distances she might have traveled in either direction. The best she could have hoped for was to marry the local Master of Fox Hounds, the worst to marry a younger son with a small farm, who probably drank. But in America she might have just as easily have been murdered by a mugger or become rich and famous. Well, she'd lost this gamble, and she didn't even have the strength to cut Philip loose. Odd that he should end up her victim, when she'd been sure the roles were reversed.

"I didn't want to become the person I am," she found herself muttering as she walked through the revolving doors into the hotel.

"Diane."

Terrific. A social encounter. Small talk. She knew herself too well to imagine she'd be rude, even in her present state of mind.

"Diane, what's the matter?"

"Hi, Mitch. Nothing. It's just the heat, I feel a little faint."

"You look terrible. I'll take you home."

"No, I was . . . I thought I'd go in and get a cold drink. Inside, it's closer."

"I'll come with you."

The bar was more than half-full. Diane had visualized somewhere empty and was grateful to Mitch. His large hand would undoubtedly leave a damp mark on her shirt, but he more than made up for it by demanding loudly, and getting, a large booth. Diane, alone, would probably have been put at a small table in the middle of the room. He ordered a large brandy for her and a glass of ice water. Both for medicinal purposes.

Mitch. Diane felt a small ray of hope. It suddenly occurred to her that he might save her. He'd once asked her to marry him and offered her a real job. Admittedly before he'd become as successful as he now was. But he seemed unchanged, so did his benevolent, kindly attitude toward her. Maybe.

"Now how do you feel?"

"Better already." And she did. "Thanks. But you were going somewhere?"

"Coming back. From my piano lesson."

"Your what? I didn't know you played the piano."

"Oh, yes. Wait until you see my apartment. There's a baby grand in the living room with no photos on it."

"But you never mentioned it before. How long have you been playing?"

"I've had six lessons. Listen, why don't you come up and I'll show you the apartment and play something for you."

He evidently caught sight of her bleak expression, because he checked himself and said:

"You probably don't feel up to it today. Being sick and everything, but we'll do it soon."

"I'd love to."

"What's wrong? Don't try and shit me."

"Nothing. I mean nothing new or specific."

"You should never have married that cold-blooded bastard."

Diane drew a deep breath. Now was the moment to undramatically describe her situation, her despair, and see if Mitch came up with any offer that might save her, or at least Philip and Tania.

But it was hard to summon the energy. And before she could, a new voice cut in:

"Don't deny it, darling. We all were so worried. All your friends, especially Claire and me, were so against it."

Claire and Sandy. Sandy's inference of friendship—of long lunches and midnight calls about Diane—was certainly more amazing than her just popping unexplained into the conversation.

"Sandy. Goodness, what're you doing here?" And, as an afterthought, remembering her manners. "You do know Mitch, don't you?"

Mitch certainly remembered who Sandy was. No two ways about that. Before Sandy could reply, he said; "Of course. We all had lunch together once." Which had been the only time they'd met, but he'd been consumed by curiosity. Always had been. A kind of prurient interest in Diane's private life, and Philip in his own right, and Sandy in hers. And all three of them in conjunction. Like his own personal soap opera.

"Sit down, sit down," he patted the banquette beside him. Sandy sat.

"Sweetie, what's the matter? You look terrible."

"Thank you. I feel terrible. You, on the contrary, look wonderful. What're you up to?"

"Oh, I'm staying here. I was with some people from San Francisco, but they had to go back early, so . . ."

Diane could easily translate that one. It was another way of saying she'd been staying at the hotel with some man, and he'd either tired of her before the prearranged period was over, or he'd booked the room (or more likely, suite) for a couple of extra days to prevent Sandy from trailing after him back to San Francisco.

205

She glanced at Mitch, no innocent in wordly matters, but failed to catch his eye. He was gaping at Sandy, only just remembering not to let his mouth drop open. Oh, honestly.

"Mitch has a keen interest in music. He's studying the piano."

"Yes, I was just telling Diane . . . Do you like music?"

"I adore it," Sandy said firmly. Diane racked her brains for any evidence, however slight, that would bear out Sandy's rather wild statement. She came up with nothing. Except that she wasn't in the mood for this.

"Listen, I've got to be going. Thanks for the drink, Mitch, and the moral and medical support."

She stood. Mitch dragged his eyes reluctantly away from Sandy.

"I'll drive you home," he said firmly, but with more kindness than enthusiasm.

"No. Mm, no, you can't. I've got to go to the market and pick up Tania from her dancing class on the way back." As she said it, she realized it was true. She'd forgotten, that was all. She'd have to hurry, or she'd be late.

"The angel, I'll stop by tomorrow if I can. Give her my love."

"Fine, I will. She's being awfully sweet. The other day I asked her to pick up her sneakers—she'd left them in the dining room—and she said, 'Why do I always have to do everything around here? Do you think I'm Cinderella and Snow White or something?' "

Mitch laughed, Sandy smiled. Diane knew it wasn't uproariously funny, but at the same time realized she thought it was adorable, Mitch thought it was cute, and Sandy was just managing a polite acknowledgement of her daughter's precocity.

If she wasn't going to leave Tania abandoned at the dancing school, she'd have to pick her up first. Then stop at the supermarket on the way home. Never mind, Tania loved that. As she moved away from the table, though her mind was elsewhere, she could hear Sandy's clear upper-class voice.

"Oh, the opera. Most of all. Why, last night I spent most of the evening listening to one of my favorites. Oh, you know, what's it called, the one about the dear little bat . . ."

Diane suddenly remembered that *Snow White* was on television that evening. She and Tania would go to Gristedes. Tania would choose her favorite supper and they'd eat it picnic-style on Diane's bed. She'd open a bottle of Philip's best wine, and maybe she'd even laugh when the movie got to "Some day my Prince will come."